P}

LS 1636a

Carole Mortimer was born in England, the youngest of three children. She began writing in 1978, and has now written over one hundred and fifty books for Harlequin Mills & Boon®. Carole has six sons: Matthew, Joshua, Timothy, Michael, David and Peter. She says, 'I'm happily married to Peter senior; we're best friends as well as lovers, which is probably the best recipe for a successful relationship. We live in a lovely part of England.'

Recent titles by the same author:

SURRENDER TO THE PAST
TAMING THE LAST ST CLAIRE
  (The Scandalous St Claires)
THE RELUCTANT DUKE
  (The Scandalous St Claires)
JORDAN ST CLAIRE: DARK AND DANGEROUS
  (The Scandalous St Claires)

Did you know these are also available as eBooks?
Visit www.millsandboon.co.uk

41	81	121	161	201	241	281	321	361	401
42	82	122	162	202	242	282	322	362	402
43	83	123	163	203	243	283	323	363	403
44	84	124	164	204	244	284	324	364	404
45	85	125	165	205	245	285	325	365	405
46	86	126	166	206	246	286	326	366	406
47	87	127	167	207	247	287	327	367	407
48	88	128	168	208	248	288	328	368	408
49	89	129	169	209	249	289	329	369	409
50	90	130	170	210	250	290	330	370	410
51	91	131	171	211	251	291	331	371	411
52	92	132	172	212	252	292	332	372	412
53	93	133	173	213	253	293	333	373	413
54	94	134	174	214	254	294	334	374	414
55	95	135	175	215	255	295	335	375	415
56	96	136	176	216	256	296	336	376	416
57	97	137	177	217	257	297	337	377	417
58	98	138	178	218	258	298	338	378	418
59	99	139	179	219	259	299	339	379	419
60	100	140	180	220	260	300	340	380	420
61	101	141	181	221	261	301	341	381	421
62	102	142	182	222	262	302	342	382	422
63	103	143	183	223	263	303	343	383	423
64	104	144	184	224	264	304	344	384	424
65	105	145	185	225	265	305	345	385	425
66	106	146	186	226	266	306	346	386	426
67	107	147	187	227	267	307	347	387	427
68	108	148	188	228	268	308	348	388	428
69	109	149	189	229	269	309	349	389	429
70	110	150	190	230	270	310	350	390	430
71	111	151	191	231	271	311	351	391	431
72	112	152	192	232	272	312	352	392	432
73	113	153	193	233	273	313	353	293	433
74	114	154	194	234	274	314	354	394	434
75	115	155	195	235	275	315	355	395	435
76	116	156	196	236	276	316	356	396	436
77	117	157	197	237	277	317	357	397	437
78	118	158	198	238	278	318	358	398	438
79	119	159	199	239	279	319	359	399	439
80	120	160	200	240	280	320	360	400	440

First published in Great Britain 2012
by Mills & Boon, an imprint of Harlequin (UK) Limited.
Harlequin (UK) Limited, Eton House, 18-24 Paradise Road,
Richmond, Surrey TW9 1SR

© Carole Mortimer 2012

ISBN: 978 0 263 22642 3

Harlequin (UK) policy is to use papers that are natural, renewable and recyclable products and made from wood grown in sustainable forests. The logging and manufacturing process conform to the legal environmental regulations of the country of origin.

Printed and bound in Great Britain
by CPI Antony Rowe, Chippenham, Wiltshire

THE TALK OF HOLLYWOOD

CHAPTER ONE

'IT WOULD appear that your guest has finally arrived, Gramps,' Stazy said as she stood stiffly beside one of the bay windows in the drawing room, facing towards the front of Bromley House and watching the sleek black sports car as it was driven down the gravel driveway of her grandfather's Hampshire estate. She was unable to make out the features of the driver of the car behind the tinted windows; but, nevertheless, she was sure that it was Jaxon Wilder, the English actor and director who for the past ten years had held the fickle world of Hollywood in the palm of his elegant hand.

'Don't be so hard on the man, Stazy; he's only five minutes late, and he did have to drive all the way from London!' her grandfather chided indulgently from the comfort of his armchair.

'Then maybe it would have been a good idea on his part to take into account the distance he had to travel and set out accordingly.' Stazy had made absolutely no secret of her disapproval of Jaxon Wilder's visit here, and found the whole idea of his wanting to write and direct a film about the life of her deceased grandmother totally unacceptable. Unfortunately, she hadn't been able to persuade her grandfather into dismissing the idea as readily—which was why Jaxon Wilder was now parking that sleek black sports car on the driveway outside her grandfather's home.

Stazy turned away before she saw the man in question alight from the car; she already knew exactly what Jaxon Wilder looked like. The whole world probably recognised Jaxon Wilder after he had completely swept the board at every awards ceremony earlier in the year with his recent film, in which he had once again acted and directed.

Aged in his mid-thirties, he was tall and lean, with wide and powerful shoulders, slightly overlong dark hair, and piercing grey eyes set either side of an aristocratic nose. His mouth was sculptured and sensual, his chin square and determined, and the deep timbre of his voice had been known to send quivers of pleasure down the spines of women of all ages. Jaxon Wilder was known to be the highest paid actor and director on both sides of the pond.

His looks and appeal had often led to his being photographed in newspapers and magazines with the latest beautiful woman to share his life—and his bed! And his reason for coming here today was to use that charm in an effort to persuade Stazy's grandfather into giving his blessing—and help—to the writing of a screenplay about the adventurous life of Stazy's grandmother, Anastasia Romanski. A woman who, as a young child, had escaped the Russian Revolution with her family by fleeing to England, and as an adult had been one of the many secret and unsung heroines of her adopted country.

Anastasia had died only two years ago, at the age of ninety-four. Her obituary in the newspaper had drawn the attention of a nosy reporter who, when he had looked deeper into Anastasia's life, had discovered that there had been far more to Anastasia Bromley than the obscure accolades mentioned. The result had been a sensationalised biography about Anastasia, published six months ago, and the ensuing publicity had caused her grandfather to suffer a mild heart attack.

In the circumstances, was it any wonder that Stazy had been horrified to discover that Jaxon Wilder intended to make a film of Anastasia's life? And, even worse, that the film director had an appointment with her grandfather in order to discuss the project? Stazy had decided it was a discussion she had every intention of being a part of!

'Sir Geoffrey.' Jaxon moved smoothly forward to shake the older man's hand as the butler showed him into the drawing room of Bromley House.

'Mr Wilder.' It was hard to believe that Geoffrey Bromley was a man aged in his mid-nineties as he returned the firmness of Jaxon's handshake. His dark hair was only lightly streaked with grey, his shoulders still stiffly erect in his tailored dark three-piece suit and snowy white shirt with a meticulously tied grey tie.

'Jaxon, please,' he invited. 'May I say how pleased I am that you agreed to see me today—?'

'Then the pleasure would appear to be all yours!'

'Stazy!' Geoffrey Bromley rebuked affectionately as he turned towards the woman who had spoken so sharply.

Jaxon turned to look at her too as she stood in front of the bay window. The sun shining in behind her made it hard for him to make out her features, although the hostility of her tone was enough of an indication that she, at least, wasn't in the least pleased by Jaxon's visit!

'My granddaughter Stazy Bromley, Mr Wilder,' Sir Geoffrey introduced lightly.

Jaxon, having refreshed his memory on the Bromley family before leaving his London hotel earlier that morning, already knew that Stazy was short for Anastasia—the same name as her grandmother. Information that had in no way prepared him for Stazy Bromley's startling resemblance to her grandmother as she stepped out of the sunlight.

About five-six in height, with the same flame-coloured hair—neither red nor gold, but a startling mixture of the two—and a pale and porcelain complexion, she had a wide, intelligent brow above sultry eyes of deep emerald-green. Her nose was small and perfectly straight, and she had full and sensuous lips above a stubbornly determined chin.

The hairstyle was different, of course; Anastasia had favoured shoulder-length hair, whereas her granddaughter's was stylishly cut in an abundance of layers that was secured at her nape and cascaded down to the middle of her back. The black, knee-length sheath of a dress she wore added to the impression of elegant chic.

Other than those minor differences Jaxon knew he might have been looking at the twenty-nine-year-old Anastasia Romanski.

Green eyes raked over Jaxon dismissively. 'Mr Wilder.'

Jaxon gave an inclination of his head. 'Miss Bromley,' he returned smoothly.

'That would be *Dr* Bromley,' she corrected coolly.

Stazy Bromley had the beauty and grace of a super-model rather than the appearance of a dusty doctor of Archaeology, as Jaxon knew her to be. Maybe, faced with her obvious antagonism towards him, Jaxon should have had Geoffrey Bromley's granddaughter investigated more thoroughly than simply making a note of her age and occupation...

'Stazy, perhaps you would like to go and tell Mrs Little we'll have tea now...?' her grandfather prompted, softly but firmly.

Those full and sensuous lips thinned. 'Is that an unsubtle hint for me to leave you and Mr Wilder alone for a few minutes, Gramps?' Stazy Bromley said dryly, those disapproving green eyes remaining firmly fixed on Jaxon.

'I think that might be best, darling,' her grandfather encouraged ruefully.

'Just try not to let Mr Wilder use his reputed charm to persuade you into agreeing to or signing anything before I get back!' she warned, with another cold glance in Jaxon's direction.

'I wouldn't dream of it, Dr Bromley,' Jaxon drawled. 'Although I'm flattered that you think I have charm!' Mockery perhaps wasn't the best line for him to take when Stazy Bromley was obviously so antagonistic towards him already, but then Jaxon couldn't say he particularly cared for being treated as if he were some sort of trickster, trying to dupe her grandfather into selling off the family jewels!

Obviously the subject of her grandmother's past was a sensitive one to Stazy Bromley.

'I don't know you well enough as yet to have decided exactly what you are, Mr Wilder,' Stazy Bromley assured him distantly.

But she obviously didn't number his 'charm' as one of his more obvious attributes, Jaxon recognised ruefully. That was a pity, because her physical similarities to her grandmother were already enough to have him intrigued. Similarities that she seemed to deliberately downplay with her lack of make-up and the confinement of her riotous red-gold hair.

If that really was Stazy's intention then she had failed miserably. As if those sultry green eyes and that poutingly sensuous mouth weren't enough of an attraction, her curvaceous figure in that fitted black dress certainly was!

Stazy had only ever seen Jaxon Wilder on the big screen before today, where he invariably appeared tall and dark and very powerful. It was an image she had believed to be magnified by the size of that screen. She had been wrong. Even dressed formally, in a tailored black suit, snowy-white silk shirt and silver tie, Jaxon Wilder was just as powerfully charismatic in the flesh.

'That really is enough, darling,' her grandfather rebuked. 'And I have no doubt that Mr Wilder and I will manage perfectly well for the short time you're gone,' he added pointedly.

'I have no doubt you will, Grandfather.' Her voice softened as she smiled affectionately at her aged grandparent before leaving.

Her grandfather was now the only family Stazy had, her parents having both died fifteen years ago, when their light aeroplane had crashed into the sea off the coast of Cornwall.

Despite already being aged in their early eighties, Anastasia and Geoffrey had been wonderful to their traumatised granddaughter, taking fourteen-year-old Stazy into their home and their lives without a second thought. As a result Stazy's protectiveness where they were both concerned was much stronger than it might otherwise have been.

To the point where she now saw Jaxon Wilder's plans to make a film about her deceased grandmother as nothing more than Hollywood sensationalism—no doubt inspired by that dreadful biography, in which her grandmother had been portrayed as the equivalent of a Russian Mata Hari working for British Intelligence!

No doubt Jaxon Wilder also saw the project as a means of earning himself yet another shelf of awards to add to his already considerable collection. That was a pity—for him!—because Stazy saw it as her mission in life to ensure that film was never made!

'I'm afraid Stazy doesn't approve of your making a film of my late wife's life, Jaxon,' Sir Geoffrey murmured wryly.

He gave a rueful smile. 'One would never have guessed!'

The older man smiled slightly. 'Please, sit down and tell me exactly what it is you want from me,' he invited smoothly as he resumed his seat in the armchair beside the unlit fireplace.

'Shouldn't we wait for your granddaughter to return before we discuss this any further?' Jaxon grimaced as he lowered his lean length down on to the chair opposite, already knowing that Stazy Bromley's attitude was going to be a problem he hadn't envisaged when he had flown over to England yesterday with the express purpose of discussing the details of the film with Geoffrey Bromley.

Jaxon had first written to the older man several months ago—a letter in which he had outlined his idea for the film. The letter he had received back from Geoffrey Bromley two weeks later had been cautiously encouraging. The two men had spoken several times on the telephone before Jaxon had suggested they meet in person and discuss the idea more extensively.

In none of those exchanges had Sir Geoffrey so much

as hinted at his granddaughter's antagonism to the film being made!

Sir Geoffrey smiled confidently. 'I assure you that ultimately Stazy will go along with whatever I decide.'

Jaxon had no doubt that when necessary the older man could be as persuasive as his wife was reputed to have been, but in a totally different way—the part Geoffrey Bromley had played in the events of the previous century were even more shrouded in mystery than those of his now deceased wife. But from the little Jaxon knew the other man had held a very high position of authority in England's security at the time of his retirement twenty-five years ago.

Was it any wonder that Stazy Bromley had the same forceful determination as both her grandparents?

Or that his own visit here today promised to be a battle of wills between the two of them!

A battle Jaxon ultimately had every intention of winning…

'I trust the two of you didn't discuss anything of importance during my absence…?' Stazy said softly as she came back into the room, closely followed by the butler. He was carrying a heavily laden silver tray, the contents of which he proceeded to place on the low coffee table in front of the sofa where Stazy now sat, looking enquiringly at the two men seated opposite.

Her grandfather gave her another of those censorious glances as Jaxon Wilder answered. 'I'm sure that neither of us would have dared to do that, Dr Bromley…' he said dryly.

Stazy was just as sure that the forceful Jaxon Wilder would pretty much dare to do anything he damn well pleased! 'Do you care for milk and sugar in your tea,

Mr Wilder?' she prompted lightly as she held the sugar bowl poised over the three delicate china cups.

'Just milk, thanks.'

Stazy nodded as she added two spoonfuls of sugar to her grandfather's cup before commencing to pour the tea. 'No doubt it becomes more difficult, as you get older, to maintain the perfect bodyweight.'

'Darling, I really don't think this constant bickering with Jaxon is necessary,' her grandfather admonished affectionately as she stood up to carry his cup and saucer over to him after handing Jaxon his own cup.

'Perhaps not,' Stazy allowed, her cheeks warming slightly at the rebuke. 'But I'm sure Mr Wilder is equally capable of defending himself if he feels it necessary.'

Jaxon was fast losing his patience with Stazy Bromley's snide comments. She might appear delicately beautiful in appearance, but as far as he could tell, where this particular woman was concerned, that was exactly where the delicacy ended.

'Undoubtedly,' he bit out abruptly. 'Now, if we could perhaps return to discussing *Butterfly*…?'

'"Butterfly"…?' his adversary repeated slowly as she resumed her seat on the sofa before crossing one silkily elegant knee over the other.

'It was your grandmother's code name—'

'I'm aware of what it was, Mr Wilder,' she cut in crisply.

'It's also the working title of my film,' Jaxon explained tersely.

'Isn't that rather presumptuous of you?' She frowned. 'As far as I'm aware,' she continued warily, 'there has been no agreement as yet to there even *being* a film, let alone it already having a working title!' She turned enquiring eyes to her grandfather, her tension palpable.

Sir Geoffrey shrugged. 'I don't believe there is any way in which we can stop Mr Wilder from making his film, Stazy.'

'But—'

'With or without our co-operation,' Sir Geoffrey added firmly. 'And personally—after the publication of that dreadful biography!—I would rather be allowed to have some say in the content than none at all.'

Stazy Bromley's eyes glittered with anger as she turned to look at Jaxon. 'If you've dared to threaten my grandfather—'

'Of course Jaxon hasn't threatened me, darling—'

'And Jaxon resents the hell—excuse my language, sir—' Jaxon nodded briefly to the older man before turning his chilling gaze back to the bristling Stazy Bromley '—out of the implication that he might have done so!'

Stazy had the good sense to realise that she just might have been out of line with that last remark. It was really no excuse that she had been predisposed to dislike Jaxon Wilder before she had even met him, based purely on the things she had read about him. Especially when he had been charm itself since his arrival. To her grandfather, at least. Stazy was pretty sure, after her barely veiled remarks, that the antagonism now went both ways!

But exactly what had Jaxon Wilder expected to happen when he had arranged to come here? That he would meet alone with a man aged in his mid-nineties who had recently suffered a heart attack? That the two of them would exchange pleasantries before he walked away with Geoffrey's complete co-operation? If that was what he'd thought was going to happen then he obviously didn't know Stazy's grandfather very well; even twenty-five years after his supposed retirement Geoffrey was a power to be reckoned with! And Stazy considered herself only one step behind him...

Not only was she a highly qualified London university lecturer, it had been hinted at by the powers that be that she was in line to become head of the department when her professor stepped down next year—and Stazy hadn't put herself in that position at only twenty-nine by being shy and retiring.

'I apologise if I was mistaken,' she murmured softly. 'Mr Wilder's use of the term "working title" seemed to imply that things had already been settled between the two of you.'

'Apology accepted,' Jaxon Wilder grated, without even the slightest lessening of the tension in those broad shoulders. 'Obviously I would rather proceed with your blessing, Sir Geoffrey.' He nodded to the older man, at the same time managing to imply that he didn't give a damn whether or not he had Stazy's!

'And his co-operation?' she put in dryly.

Cool grey eyes turned back in her direction. 'Of course.'

Stazy repressed the shiver that threatened to run the length of her spine—of alarm rather than the pleasure she imagined most women felt when Jaxon Wilder looked at them! As his icy gaze raked over her with slow criticism Stazy knew exactly what he would see: a woman who preferred a no-nonsense appearance. Her lashes were naturally long and dark, requiring no mascara, and in fact her face was completely bare of makeup apart from a pale peach lipgloss. Her hands, throat and ears were completely unadorned with jewellery.

Certainly Stazy knew herself to be nothing in the least like the beautiful and willowy actresses in whose company Jaxon Wilder had so often been seen, photographed for newspapers and magazines during the last dozen years or so. She doubted the man would even know what to do with an intelligent woman...

What on earth—?

Why should she care what Jaxon Wilder thought of her? As far as Stazy was concerned there would be absolutely no reason for the two of them ever to meet again after today—let alone for her to care what he thought of her as a woman...

She straightened determinedly. 'I believe you are not only wasting your own time, Mr Wilder, but also my grandfather's and mine—'

'As it happens, I'm willing to give Jaxon my blessing and my co-operation. I will allow him to read letters and personal papers of Anastasia's.' Geoffrey spoke firmly over Stazy's scathing dismissal. 'But only under certain conditions.'

Stazy's eyes widened as she turned to look at her grandfather. 'You can't be serious!'

Her grandfather gave a slight inclination of his head. 'I believe you will find, darling, that it's called controlling a situation that one knows is inevitable, rather than attempting a futile fight against it.'

Jaxon felt none of the exhilaration he might have expected to feel at Sir Geoffrey not only giving his blessing to the making of the film, but also offering him access to certain of Anastasia's personal papers in order to aid in the writing of the screenplay. Inwardly he sensed that whatever Geoffrey's conditions were, Jaxon wasn't going to like them...

Stazy Bromley obviously felt that same sense of unease as she stood up abruptly, a frown between those clear green eyes as she stared down at her grandfather for several long seconds before her expression softened slightly.

'Darling, remember what happened after that awful book was published—'

'I'm insulted that you would even *think* of comparing the film I intend to make with that sensationalised trash!' Jaxon rose sharply to his feet.

She turned to look at him coolly. 'How can I think otherwise?'

'Maybe by giving me a chance—'

'Now, now, you two.' Sir Geoffrey chuckled softly. 'It really doesn't bode well if the two of you can't even be in the same room together without arguing.'

Jaxon's earlier feeling of trepidation grew as he turned to look down at the older man, not fooled for a moment by the innocence of Sir Geoffrey's expression. 'Perhaps you would care to explain your conditions…?' he prompted slowly, warily. Whatever ace Geoffrey Bromley had hidden up his sleeve Jaxon was utterly convinced he wasn't going to like it!

The older man gave a shrug. 'My first condition is that there will be no copies made of my wife's personal papers. In fact they are never to leave this house.'

That was going to make things slightly awkward. It would mean that Jaxon would have to spend several days—possibly a week—here at Bromley House in order to read those papers and make notes before he was able to go away and write the screenplay. But, busy schedule permitting, there was no real reason why it couldn't be done. Over the years he had certainly stayed in infinitely less salubrious places than the elegant comfort of Bromley House!

'My second condition—'

'Exactly how many conditions are there?' Jaxon prompted with amusement.

'Just the two,' Sir Geoffrey assured him dryly. 'And the first condition will only apply if you agree to the second.'

'Fine.' Jaxon nodded ruefully.

'Oh, I wouldn't give me your agreement just yet, Jaxon,' the older man warned derisively.

Stazy didn't at all like the calculating glint she could clearly see in her grandfather's eyes. His first condition made a certain amount of sense—although there was no guarantee, of course. But at least Jaxon Wilder having access to her grandmother's personal papers might mean there was a slight chance his screenplay would have some basis in truth. Not much, but some.

That only left her grandfather's second condition…

'Go ahead, Gramps,' she invited softly.

'Perhaps you should both sit down first…?'

Stazy tensed and at the same time sensed Jaxon's own increased wariness as he stood across the room from her. 'Do we need to sit down…?'

'Oh I think it might be advisable,' her grandfather confirmed dryly.

'I'll remain standing, if you don't mind,' Jaxon Wilder rasped gruffly.

'Not at all,' Geoffrey chuckled. 'Stazy?'

'The same,' she murmured warily.

'Very well.' Her grandfather relaxed back in his chair as he looked up at the two of them. 'I have found your conversation today highly…diverting, shall we say? And I assure you there is really very little that a man of my age finds in the least amusing!' her grandfather added ruefully.

He was playing with them, Stazy recognised frustratedly. Amusing himself at their expense. 'Will you just spit it out, Gramps!'

He smiled slightly as he rested his elbows on the arms of the chair before linking his fingers together in front of his chest. 'Stazy, you obviously have reservations about the content of Jaxon's film—'

'With good reason!'

'With no reason whatsoever,' Jaxon corrected grimly. 'I am not the one responsible for that dreadful biography—nor have I ever written or starred in a film that twists the truth in order to add sensationalism,' he added hardly.

'I doubt most Hollywood actors would recognise the truth if it jumped up and bit them on the nose!' Those green eyes glittered with scorn.

Jaxon wasn't sure which one of them had closed the distance between them—was only aware that they now stood so close that their noses were almost touching as she glared up at him and Jaxon scowled right back down at her.

He was suddenly aware of the soft insidiousness of Stazy's perfume: a heady combination of cinnamon, lemon and—much more disturbing—hotly enraged woman…

Close to her like this, Jaxon could see that those amazing green eyes had a ring of black about the iris, giving them a strangely luminous quality that was almost mesmerising when fringed with the longest, darkest lashes he had ever seen. Her complexion was the pale ivory of fine bone china, with the same delicacy of appearance.

A delicacy that was completely at odds with the sensual fullness of her mouth.

Her lips were slightly parted now, to reveal small and perfectly straight white teeth. Small white teeth that Jaxon imagined could bite a man with passion as easily as— What the…?

Jaxon stepped back abruptly as he realised he had allowed his thoughts to wander way off the reservation, considering the antagonism the two of them clearly felt towards each other. Not only that, but Stazy Bromley was exactly like all the buttoned-down and career-orientated women he knew who had clawed themselves up the professional ladder so that they might inhabit the higher echelons of certain film studios. Hard, unfeminine women, whom Jaxon always avoided like the plague!

He eased the tension from his shoulders before turning back to face the obviously still amused Geoffrey Bromley. 'I agree with Stazy—'

'How refreshing!' she cut in dryly.

'You may as well just get this is over with,' Jaxon finished ruefully.

'Let's hope the two of you are in as much agreement about my second condition.' Sir Geoffrey nodded, no longer smiling or as relaxed as he had been a short time ago. 'I've given the matter some thought, and in view of Stazy's lack of enthusiasm for the making of your film, and your own obvious determination to prove her suspicions wrong, Jaxon, I feel it would be better for all concerned if Stazy were to assist you in collating and researching Anastasia's personal papers.'

'What…?'

Jaxon was completely in agreement with Stazy Bromley's obvious horror at the mere suggestion of the two of them working that closely together even for one minute, let alone the days or weeks it might take him to go through Anastasia Bromley's papers!

CHAPTER TWO

STAZY was the first to recover her powers of speech. 'You can't be serious, Gramps—'

'I assure you I am perfectly serious.' He nodded gravely.

She gave a disbelieving shake of her head. 'I can't just take time off from the university whenever I feel like it!'

'I'm sure Jaxon won't mind waiting a few weeks until you finish for the long summer break.'

'But I've been invited to join a dig in Iraq this summer—'

'And I sincerely doubt that any of those artifacts having already been there for hundreds if not thousands of years, are going to disappear overnight just because you arrive a week later than expected,' her grandfather reasoned pleasantly.

Stazy stared down at him in complete frustration, knowing that she owed both him and her grandmother so much more than a week of her time. That if it wasn't for the two of them completely turning their own lives upside down fifteen years ago she would never have coped with her parents deaths as well as she had. It had also been their encouragement and support that had helped her through an arduous university course and then achieving her doctorate.

Stazy's thoughts came to an abrupt halt as she suddenly became aware of Jaxon Wilder's unnatural silence.

Those silver-grey eyes were narrowed on her grandfather, hard cheekbones thrown into sharp prominence by the clenching of his jaw, and his mouth was a thin and uncompromising line. His hands too were clenched, into fists at his sides.

Obviously not a happy bunny, either, Stazy recognised ruefully.

Although any satisfaction she might have felt at that realisation was totally nullified by her own continued feelings of horror at her grandfather's proposal. 'I believe you will find Mr Wilder is just as averse to the idea as I am, Gramps,' she drawled derisively.

He shrugged. 'Then it would appear to be a case of film and be damned,' he misquoted softly.

Stazy drew in a sharp breath as she remembered the furore that had followed the publication of the unauthorised biography six months ago. The press had hounded her grandfather for weeks afterwards—to the extent that he had arranged for round-the-clock guards to be placed at Bromley House and his house in London. And he had suffered a heart attack because of the emotional strain he had been put under.

Stazy had even had one inventive reporter sit in on one of her lectures without detection, only to corner her with a blast of personal questions at the end—much to her embarrassment and anger.

The thought of having to go through all that again was enough to send cold shivers of dread down Stazy's spine. 'Perhaps you might somehow persuade Mr Wilder into not making the film at all, Gramps?' Although her own behaviour towards him this past hour or so certainly wasn't conducive to Jaxon Wilder wanting to do her any favours!

Probably she should have thought of that earlier. Her grandmother had certainly believed in the old adage, 'You'll catch more with honey than with vinegar...'

The derision in Jaxon Wilder's piercing grey eyes as he looked at her seemed to indicate he was perfectly aware of Stazy's belated regrets! 'What form of...persuasion did you have in mind, Dr Bromley?' he drawled mockingly.

Stazy felt the colour warm her cheeks. 'I believe I referred to my grandfather's powers of persuasion rather than my own,' she returned irritably.

'Pity,' he murmured softly, those grey eyes speculative as his gaze moved slowly over Stazy, from her two-inch-heeled shoes, her curvaceous figure in the black dress, to the top of her flame-coloured head, before settling on the pouting fullness of her mouth.

She frowned her irritation as she did her best to ignore that blatantly sexual gaze. 'Surely you can appreciate how much the making of this film is going to upset my grandfather?'

'On the contrary.' Jaxon deeply resented Stazy Bromley's tone. 'I believe that a film showing the true events of seventy years ago can only be beneficial to your grandmother's memory.'

'Oh, please, Mr Wilder.' Stazy Bromley eyed him pityingly. 'We both know that your only interest in making this particular film is in going up on that stage in a couple of years' time to collect yet another batch of awards!'

Jaxon drew in a sharp breath. 'You—'

'Enough!' Sir Geoffrey firmly cut in on the conversation before Jaxon had chance to finish his blistering reply. Eyes of steely-blue raked over both of them as he stood up. 'I believe that for the moment I have heard quite enough on this subject from both of you.' He gave an impatient shake of his head. 'You'll be staying for dinner, I hope, Jaxon…?' He raised steel-grey brows questioningly.

'If you feel we can make any progress by my doing so—yes, of course I'll stay to dinner,' Jaxon bit out tensely.

Sir Geoffrey gave a derisive smile. 'I believe it will be up to you and Stazy as to whether any progress will or can be made before you leave here later today,' he said dryly. 'And, with that in mind, I am going upstairs to take a short nap before dinner. Stazy, perhaps you would like to take Mr Wilder for a walk in the garden while I'm gone? My roses are particularly lovely this year, Jaxon, and their perfume is strongest in the late afternoon and early evening,' he added lightly, succeeding in silencing his granddaughter as she drew in another deep breath with the obvious intention of arguing against his suggestion.

Jaxon was reminded that the older man had once been in a position of control over the whole of British Intelligence, let alone one stubbornly determined granddaughter! 'A walk in the garden sounds…pleasant,' Jaxon answered noncommittally, not completely sure that Stazy Bromley wouldn't use the opportunity to try and stab him with a garden fork while they were outside, and so put an end to this particular problem.

'That's settled, then,' Sir Geoffrey said heartily. 'Do cheer up, darling.' He bent to kiss his granddaughter on the forehead. 'I very much doubt that Jaxon has any intention of attempting to steal the family silver before he leaves!'

The sentiment was so close to Jaxon's own earlier thoughts in regard to Stazy's obviously scathing opinion of him that he couldn't help but chuckle wryly. 'No, Sir Geoffrey, I believe you may rest assured that all your family jewels are perfectly safe where I'm concerned.'

The older man placed an affectionate arm about his granddaughter's slender shoulders. 'Stazy is the only family jewel I care anything about, Jaxon.'

'In that case, they're most *definitely* safe!' Jaxon assured him with hard dismissal.

'And on that note…' Sir Geoffrey smiled slightly as his arm dropped back to his side. 'I'll see both of you in a couple of hours.' He turned and left the room. Leaving a tense and awkward silence behind him…

Stazy was very aware of the barely leashed power of the man walking beside her across the manicured lawn in the warmth of the late-afternoon sunshine, and could almost feel the heated energy radiating off Jaxon Wilder. Or perhaps it was just repressed anger? The two of them had certainly got off to a bad start earlier—and it had only become worse during the course of the next hour!

Mainly because of her own less-than-pleasant attitude, Stazy accepted. But what else had this man expected? That she was just going to stand by and risk her grandfather becoming ill again?

She gave a weary sigh before breaking the silence between them. 'Perhaps we should start again, Mr Wilder?'

He raised dark brows as he looked down at her. 'Perhaps we should, Dr Bromley?'

'Stazy,' she invited abruptly.

'Jaxon,' he drawled in return.

He obviously wasn't going to make this easy for her, Stazy acknowledged impatiently. 'I'm sure you are aware of what happened five months ago, and why I now feel so protective towards my grandfather?'

'Of course.' Jaxon gave a rueful smile as he ducked beneath the trailing branches of a willow tree, only to discover there was a wooden swing chair beneath the vibrant green leaves. 'Shall we…?' he prompted lightly. 'I resent the fact,' he continued once they were both seated, 'that you believe he might need any protection from me.'

That was fair enough, Stazy acknowledged grudgingly. Except she still believed this man was in a position to cause her grandfather unnecessary distress. 'He and my grandmother were totally in love with each other until the very end…'

Jaxon heard clearly the pain of loss underlying her statement. 'I'm not about to do anything to damage either Geoffrey's or your own treasured memories of Anastasia,' he assured her huskily.

'No?'

'No,' Jaxon said evenly. 'On the contrary—I'm hoping my film will help to set the record straight where your grandmother's actions seventy years ago are concerned. I don't believe in making money—or in acquiring awards—' he gave her a pointed look '—by causing someone else unnecessary pain.'

Stazy felt her cheeks warm at the rebuke. 'Perhaps we should just draw a veil over our previous conversation, Jaxon…?'

'Perhaps we should.' He chuckled wryly.

Stazy's eyes widened as she saw that a cleft had appeared in Jaxon's left cheek as he smiled, and those grey eyes were no longer cold but the warm colour of liquid mercury, his teeth very white and even against his lightly tanned skin.

Stazy had spent the past eleven years acquiring her degree, her doctorate, and lecturing—as well as attending as many archaeological digs around the world as she could during the holidays. Leaving very little time for such frivolities as attending the cinema. Even so, she had seen several of Jaxon Wilder's films, and was able to appreciate that the man in the flesh was very much more...*immediate* than even his sexy screen image portrayed. Mesmerisingly so...

Just as she was aware of the heat of his body as he sat beside her on the swing seat—of the way his lightly spicy aftershave intermingled with the more potent and earthy smell of a virile male in his prime.

That was something of an admission from a woman who over the years had eschewed even the suggestion of a personal relationship in favour of concentrating on her career. And now certainly wasn't the time for Stazy to belatedly develop a crush on a film star!

Even one as suavely handsome as Jaxon Wilder...

Especially one as suavely handsome as Jaxon Wilder! What could a London university lecturer in archaeology and an award-winning Hollywood actor/director possibly have in common? *Nothing*, came the clear answer!

Was she disappointed at that realisation? No, of course she wasn't! Was she...?

Stazy got abruptly to her feet. 'Shall we continue with our walk?' She set out determinedly towards the fishpond, without so much as waiting to see if he followed her.

Jaxon slowly stood to stroll along behind Stazy, not quite sure what had happened to make her take off so abruptly, only knowing that something had. He also knew, after years of spending time with women who were totally fixated on both their career and their appearance—and not necessarily in that order!—that Stazy Bromley was so much more complex than that. An enigma. One that was starting to interest him in spite of himself, Jaxon acknowledged ruefully as he realised he was watching the way her perfectly rounded bottom moved sensuously beneath her black fitted dress as she walked…

Even Stazy's defence of her grandparents, although an irritation to him, and casting aspersions upon his own character as it undoubtedly did, was still a trait to be admired. Most of the women Jaxon was acquainted with would sell their soul to the devil—let alone their grandparents' reputations!—if it meant they could attract even a little publicity for themselves by doing so!

Stazy Bromley obviously did the opposite. Even that inaccurate biography had only fleetingly mentioned that Anastasia had had one child and one grandchild, and any attempt to talk to Stazy after the publication of that book had been met with the response that 'Dr Stazy Bromley does not give personal interviews'.

'So,' Jaxon began as he joined her beside a pond full of large golden-coloured fish, 'what do you think of your grandfather's idea that the two of us meet here in the summer and research your grandmother's personal papers together…?'

She gave a humourless smile as she continued to watch the fish lazing beneath the water in the warmth of the early-evening sunshine. 'If I didn't know better I would say it was the onset of senility!'

Jaxon chuckled appreciatively. 'But as we both do know better…?'

She gave a shrug. 'You really can't be persuaded into dropping the film idea altogether?'

He drew in a sharp breath. 'Stazy, even if I said yes I know for a fact that there are at least two other directors with an interest in making their own version of what happened.'

Stazy turned to look at him searchingly, knowing by the openness of his expression as he returned her gaze that he was telling her the truth. 'Directors who may not have your integrity?' she questioned flatly.

'Probably not.' He grimaced.

'So, what you're saying is it's a question of going with the devil we know, or allowing some other film director to totally blacken my grandmother's name and reputation?' Stazy guessed heavily.

Jaxon nodded abruptly. 'That about sums it up, yes.'

Damned if they did—double damned it they didn't. 'You do realise that if I agree to do this I would be doing so under protest?'

His mouth twisted derisively. 'Oh, I believe you've made your feelings on that particular subject more than clear, Stazy,' he assured her dryly.

She shot him an irritated glance before once again turning to walk away, this time in the direction of the horses grazing in a corner of the meadow that adjoined the garden. One of those horses, a beautiful chestnut stallion, ambled over to stretch its neck across the fence, so that Stazy could stroke absently down the long length of his nose as she continued to consider the options available to her.

There really weren't any.

She either agreed to help Jaxon Wilder in his research or she refused, and then he'd go ahead and make the film without any input from her grandfather or Anastasia's private papers.

Her uncharacteristic physical awareness of this man was not only unacceptable but also baffling to Stazy, and even now, standing just feet away from him as she continued to stroke Copper's nose, she was totally aware of Jaxon's disturbing presence. Too much for her not to know that spending a week in his company was simply asking for trouble.

It was all too easy for Jaxon to see the riot of emotions that flashed across Stazy Bromley's expressive face as she considered what to do about this situation: impatience, frustration, anger, dismay—

Dismay…?

Jaxon raised dark brows as he wondered what *that* was all about. Obviously Stazy would rather this situation didn't exist at all, but she didn't appear to be the type of woman who would allow anything to get the better of her… And exactly *why* was he even bothering to wonder what type of woman Stazy Bromley was? Jaxon questioned self-derisively.

Her physical resemblance to her grandmother had aroused his interest initially, but this last hour or so of being insulted by her—both for who and what he was— had surely nullified that initial spark of appreciation?

Jaxon studied Stazy from beneath lowered lids. That wonderful hair gleamed fiery-gold in the sunlight, her eyes were a sultry and luminescent green, and there was a slight flush to her cheeks from walking in the sunshine. Her full and sensuous lips curved into an affectionate smile as the stallion nudged against her shoulder for attention.

He drew in a deep breath. 'It must have been a difficult time for you after your parents died—'

'I would rather not discuss my own private life with you, if you don't mind,' she said stiffly.

'I was only going to say that this must have been a wonderful place to spend your teenage years,' Jaxon murmured as he turned to lean his elbows on the fence and look across at the mellow-stoned house.

'It was—yes,' Stazy confirmed huskily. She looked up at him curiously. 'Whereabouts in England are you from?'

'Cambridgeshire.'

'And do you still go home?' she prompted curiously.

'Whenever I can.' Jaxon nodded. 'Which probably isn't as often as my family would like. My parents and younger brother still live in the small village where I grew up. But it's nowhere near as nice as this.'

It really was idyllic here, Jaxon appreciated, with horses gently grazing behind them, birds singing in the trees in the beautiful wooded area surrounding Bromley House and the coastline edging onto the grounds. The slightly salty smell of the sea was just discernible as waves gently rose and fell on the distant sand.

'I had forgotten that places like this existed,' he added almost wistfully.

'Nothing like it in LA, hmm?' Stazy mocked as she turned to look at him.

He shot her a rueful smile. 'Not exactly, no.' The place he had bought on the coast in Malibu several years ago was too huge and modern to feel in the least homely. 'Although I do own a place in New England—very rustic and in the woods—where I go whenever I get the chance.' Which, he realised, hadn't been all that often during recent years...

He had been busy filming and then editing his last film most of the previous year, then caught up in attending the premieres and numerous awards ceremonies since—including those that Stazy had mocked earlier! All of that had left him little time in which to sit back and smell the roses. Here at Bromley House it was possible to do that. Literally.

But the serpent in this particular Eden appeared to be the tangible antagonism of the beautiful and strangely alluring woman standing beside him…

Jaxon breathed deeply. 'For your grandfather's sake, couldn't we at least try to—?' He broke off as Stazy gave a derisive laugh. 'What?' he prompted irritably.

'My grandfather has taught me never to trust any statement that begins with "for whoever or whatever's sake"!' she revealed. 'He assures me it's usually a prefix to someone imposing their will by the use of emotional blackmail!'

Jaxon gave a rueful shake of his head. 'I would have thought you were old enough to make up your own mind about another person's intentions!'

Stazy felt the sting of colour in her cheeks at this obvious challenge. 'Oh, I am, Jaxon,' she assured him derisively.

He arched dark brows. 'And you decided I was going to be trouble before you even met me?' he guessed easily.

'Yes.' A belief that had been more than borne out these past few minutes as Stazy had become more physically aware of this magnetically handsome man in a way she wasn't in the least comfortable with! 'Shall we go back to the house?' It was a rhetorical and terse suggestion on Stazy's part, and she gave Copper one last affectionate stroke on his velvet-soft nose before walking away.

Jaxon fell into step beside her seconds later. 'And is that your final word on the subject?'

Stazy eyed him derisively. 'Don't be misled by my grandfather's social graciousness or his age, Jaxon. If you do come here to stay for a week to do your research then I believe you will very quickly learn that he always has the last word on any subject!'

Jaxon Wilder wouldn't be here at all if Stazy had her way!

A fact he was well aware of if his rueful smile was any indication. He shrugged those impossibly wide shoulders. 'Then I guess the outcome of all this is completely in your grandfather's hands.'

'Yes,' she acknowledged heavily, knowing her grandfather had left her in no doubt earlier as to what he had already decided…

Geoffrey was his usual charming self when he returned downstairs a short time later, obviously refreshed and alert from his nap. He took charge of the conversation as they all ate what on the surface appeared to be a leisurely dinner together.

Beneath that veneer of politeness it was a different matter, of course: Stazy still viewed Jaxon Wilder with suspicion; and on his part she was sure there was amusement, at her expense, glittering in those mercurial grey eyes every time he so much as glanced her in her direction!

By the time they reached the coffee stage of the meal Stazy could cheerfully have screamed at the underlying tension in the air that surrounded them.

'So.' Her grandfather finally sat back in his chair at the head of the table. 'Did the two of you manage to come to any sort of compromise in my absence?'

Jaxon gave a derisive smile as he saw the way Stazy's mouth had thinned into stubbornness. 'I believe my conclusion is that all the talking in the world between the two of us won't make the slightest bit of difference when you are the one to have the final say in the matter!'

'Indeed?' the older man drawled. 'Is that what you believe, too, Stazy?'

She shrugged slender shoulders. 'You know that I will go along with whatever you decide, Gramps.'

'I would rather have your co-operation, darling,' Geoffrey prompted gently.

Jaxon watched Stazy from beneath lowered lids as he took a sip of his brandy, knowing her initial antagonism towards him hadn't lessened at all over the hours. That if anything Stazy seemed even more wary of him now than she had been earlier—to the point where she had avoided even looking at him for the past half an hour or so, let alone making conversation with him.

Could that possibly be because she was as physically aware of him as Jaxon was of her...?

Doubtful!

She grimaced before answering her grandfather. 'Mr Wilder has very kindly pointed out to me that he isn't the only film director interested in making a film about Granny.' The coldness of Stazy's tone implied she considered Jaxon anything but kind.

'So I believe, yes.' Geoffrey nodded.

Stazy's eyes widened. 'You knew that?'

'Of course I knew, darling,' her grandfather dismissed briskly. 'I may not be in the thick of things nowadays, but I still make it my business to know of anything of concern to my family or myself.'

Jaxon frowned. 'In my defence, I would like you to

know that I have every intention of giving a fair and truthful version of the events of seventy years ago.'

'You wouldn't be here at all if I wasn't already well aware of that fact, Jaxon.' Steely-blue eyes met his unblinkingly. 'If I had believed you were anything less than a man of integrity I would never have spoken to you on the telephone, let alone invited you into my home.'

His respect and liking for the older man deepened. 'Thank you.'

'Oh, don't thank me too soon.' Sir Geoffrey smiled. 'I assure you, you've yet to convince my granddaughter!' he drawled, with an affectionate glance at Stazy's less than encouraging expression.

Jaxon grimaced. 'Perhaps the situation might change once we've worked together…?'

'Stazy…?' Geoffrey said softly.

Stazy was totally aware of being the focus of both men's gazes as they waited for her to answer—her grandfather's encouraging, Jaxon Wilder's much more guarded as he watched her through narrowed lids.

But what choice did she have, really…?

Her own feelings aside, her grandfather might have said he would have to accept Jaxon's film and 'be damned', but Stazy wasn't fooled for a moment. She knew of her grandfather's deep and abiding love for her grandmother, and of how much it would hurt him—perhaps fatally—if the film about Anastasia were to be in any way defamatory. And the only way to guarantee that didn't happen was if she agreed to work with Jaxon Wilder.

'Okay,' Stazy agreed heavily. 'I can give you precisely one week of my time at the beginning of my summer break.' She glared across at Jaxon as she recognised the triumphant gleam that had flared in his gaze at her capitulation. 'But only on the condition.'

'Another condition?' Jaxon grimaced.

She nodded. 'My grandfather has to give his full approval of the screenplay once it's been written,' she added firmly.

Working here with the prickly Stazy Bromley for a week was far from ideal as far as Jaxon was concerned. But not impossible when he considered the alternative…

'Fine.' He nodded abrupt agreement.

The tension visibly left Sir Geoffrey's shoulders, and Stazy saw this as evidence that he hadn't been as relaxed about this situation as he wished to appear. 'In that case, shall we expect to see you back here the first week of July, Jaxon?'

'Yes.' Even if that would involve reshuffling his schedule in order to fit in with Stazy Bromley's.

She still looked far from happy about the arrangement…

Her next comment only confirmed it. 'A word of warning, though, Jaxon—if anything happens to my grandfather because of this film then I am going to hold you totally responsible!'

Great.

Just great!

CHAPTER THREE

'WHAT'S with all the extra security at the front gates?'

Much as six weeks previously, Stazy had been prowling restlessly up and down in the drawing room of Bromley House as she waited for Jaxon Wilder. Her stomach had tightened into knots when she'd finally seen their visitor had arrived. Not in the expensive black sports car she had been expecting, but on a powerful black and chrome motorbike instead.

Convinced Jaxon Wilder couldn't possibly be the person riding that purring black machine, and confused as to why the guards had let a biker through the front gates at all, Stazy had continued to frown out of the window as the rider had brought the bike to a halt outside the drawing room window, before swinging off the seat and straightening to his full, impressive height.

The man was completely dressed in black—black helmet with smoky-black visor, black leathers that fitted snugly to muscled shoulders and back, narrowed waist and taut backside, and long, powerful legs. Black leather gloves. And heavy black biker boots.

He—it was definitely a he, with that height and those wide and muscled shoulders—had had his back turned towards her as he'd removed his gloves, before unfastening and removing the helmet and shaking back his almost shoulder-length dark hair as he placed the helmet on top of the black leather seat.

Stazy had felt the colour drain from her cheeks as the rider had turned and she had instantly recognised him. Jaxon Wilder. Almost instantly he had looked straight up into the window where she stood staring down at him, leaving her in absolutely no doubt as to his knowing he was being watched.

Staring?

Gaping at him was probably a more apt description!

All her defences had gone—crumbled—with the disappearance of the sophisticated man she had met six weeks ago, wearing a discreetly tailored suit, silk shirt and tie, with his dark hair slightly long but nevertheless neatly styled. In his place was a rugged and dangerous-looking man who looked as if he would be completely at home at a Hell's Angels reunion!

Stazy had left all the details of Jaxon's visit to her grandfather, knowing from conversations with Geoffrey that the two men had been in contact by telephone on several occasions during the last six weeks, and that the date for Jaxon to arrive at Bromley House had been fixed for today—the day after Stazy had driven herself down from London.

That initial meeting with Jaxon, the sizzling awareness she had felt, had seemed like something of a dream once Stazy had been back in London. So much so that she hadn't even mentioned her encounter to any of her friends at the university. Besides, she very much doubted that her work colleagues would have been interested in knowing she had spent part of the weekend with the famous Hollywood actor and director Jaxon Wilder.

But that didn't mean Stazy hadn't thought about him.

About the way he looked. The aura of male power that was so much a part of him. The mesmerising grey of his eyes. The sensual curve of those chiselled lips. The deep and sexy timbre of his voice...

That aura was even more in evidence today—dangerously so!—as he looked up at her and gave her a slow and knowing grin.

Stazy had been completely flustered at being caught staring at him. Damn it, just because the man had arrived today looking like testosterone on legs, it didn't mean she had to behave as though she were no older than one of her students. She was virtually drooling, with her tongue almost hanging out, and she found it impossible to look away from how hot Jaxon looked in biker's leathers!

He had become no less imposing when the butler had shown him into the drawing room. Those leathers fitted Jaxon's muscled body like a second skin, the black boots added a couple of inches to his already considerable height, and that overlong dark hair fell softly onto his shoulders.

Already feeling something of a fool for being caught staring out of the window at him in that ridiculous way, Stazy was in no mood to repeat the experience.

'And a good afternoon to you, too, Jaxon,' she drawled pointedly.

Humour lightened his eyes. 'Are we aiming at playing nice this time around?'

'I thought we might give it a try, yes.' The tartness in her voice totally belied that.

Jaxon grinned, totally appreciative of how good Stazy looked in a white blouse that fitted snugly to the flatness of her abdomen and the fullness of her breasts, with faded denims fitting just as snugly to her curvaceous bottom and long and slender legs. Her glorious red-gold hair tumbled in loose layers over her shoulders and down the slenderness of her back today. And those sultry green eyes glowed like twin emeralds in the sun-kissed beauty of her delicately beautiful face.

She looked far younger and sexier today than the twenty-nine Jaxon knew her to be. In fact if any of his own university lecturers had ever looked this good then he doubted he would ever have been able to concentrate on attaining his degree. 'In that case, good afternoon, Stazy,' he drawled.

She gave him a slow and critical perusal, from the soles of his booted feet to his overlong hair. 'Are you on your way to a fancy dress party?'

He raised derisive brows. 'Whatever happened to playing nice…?'

She shrugged. 'It seems a perfectly reasonable question, considering the way you're dressed today. Or not, as the case may be.' She grimaced.

After the way she had stared wide-eyed at him out of the window earlier, Jaxon wasn't at all convinced by Dr Stazy Bromley's condescending tone in regard to the way he was dressed. He returned her shrug. 'I keep an apartment for my use when I'm in London, and the car and the bike are kept there too. As it's such a beautiful day, and I've been stuck on a plane for hours, I decided a ride down on the bike was called for.' He gave an appreciative smile. 'Have you ever been on a bike before, Stazy?'

'No,' Stazy answered huskily, her cheeks blazing with colour as she was assailed with the idea of wrapping her legs around that monstrous machine, feeling its vibration between her legs even as her arms were tightly clasped about the strength of Jaxon's waist, her breasts pressed against the warmth of that muscled back—

'Would you like to…?'

Stazy straightened abruptly, completely nonplussed at the way her thoughts kept wandering down a sensual path that was totally alien to her. Especially as she had managed to convince herself these last six weeks that she had imagined finding this man in the least attractive! 'No, thanks,' she dismissed coolly.

'You only have to say so if you should change your mind…'

'I won't,' she assured firmly. 'Is the bike also the reason for the long hair?' she prompted abruptly, fighting the uncharacteristic longing to run her fingers through those silky dark locks…

She had dated very little during the past eleven years, and the few men she had been out with had always possessed intellect rather than brawn. She had never particularly cared for long hair on men—had always thought it rather effeminate.

Jaxon had shown on the last occasion they had met that he was a man of intellect as well as brawn. And as for his being effeminate—the man was so blatantly male there was no possibility of ever doubting his masculinity!

'The long hair is for a pirate movie I start filming next month.' He ran his fingers ruefully through the length of that hair.

In exactly the same way Stazy's fingers itched to do!

She clasped her wayward hands firmly together behind her back. 'I'd always assumed actors wore a wig or extensions for those sorts of roles?'

He grimaced. 'I've always preferred to go with the real thing.'

Just the thought of Jaxon as a pirate, sweeping his captive—*her*!—up into his arms, was enough to make Stazy's palms feel damp. 'Whatever,' she snapped.

What on earth was wrong with her?

She'd never had fantasies about being swept off her feet by a marauding pirate before, so why now?

The disturbing answer to that question unfortunately stood only feet away from her...

'So, you didn't answer me—what's with the added security at the front gates?' Jaxon prompted lightly.

'I'm afraid it's all over the estate—not just the front gates.' Stazy shrugged. 'My grandfather arranged it.'

That didn't sound good. 'To keep the two of us in or other people out?' he asked.

'Very funny.' Those full and sensuous lips thinned at his teasing. 'Gramps received a telephone call late last night and the security guards arrived almost immediately afterwards. I believe he did attempt to call you and give you the option to postpone your visit until a later date, but he couldn't reach you on any of the telephone numbers you'd given him...' She arched red-gold brows.

'As I said earlier, I only arrived in England a few hours ago. I was probably in transit,' Jaxon dismissed distractedly. 'Any idea what the problem is?'

'Gramps never discusses matters of security with me.' She shook her head. 'Unfortunately you won't be able to discuss it with him either,' she added unapologetically, 'because he left for London very early this morning.'

Meaning that, apart from the household staff, the two of them were currently alone here together.

Probably not a good idea, when Jaxon was totally aware of Stazy's femininity today in the fitted blouse and tight denims. And that glorious unconfined red-gold hair was a temptation he was barely able to resist reaching out and touching.

What would it feel like, he wondered, to entangle his fingers in that silky hair? Or, even more appealing, to have the length of that gorgeous hair tumbling sensuously about his thighs as a naked Stazy knelt between his parted legs, her fingers curled about his throbbing shaft as she bent forward to taste him…?

'He did say he would try to telephone you later today to explain,' she added dismissively.

'Fine,' Jaxon accepted tersely, aware that his erotic imaginings had produced a bulge of arousal beneath the fitted leathers. Something Stazy was going to become aware of too if he didn't get out of here soon!

'I'm sure he'll understand if, under the circumstances, you decide you would rather leave the research for now and come back another time…'

Was that hope he heard in Stazy's voice? Probably, Jaxon acknowledged ruefully. Despite her casual appearance, she didn't seem any more pleased to see him this time around than she had six weeks ago. 'Sorry to disappoint you, Stazy, but I don't have any other time free.'

'I assure you it makes absolutely no difference to me whether you stay or go,' she dismissed scathingly.

Nope, Stazy wasn't pleased to have him here at all. 'In that case, I'm staying,' he drawled.

Stazy nodded tersely. 'Gramps left all the necessary papers in the library for us to look through, if you would like to get started?'

Jaxon shook his head. 'I've been travelling for almost twenty-four hours. What I would really like to do is shower and change out of these leathers.' All of that should give enough time for his wayward arousal to ease!

Unfortunately Jaxon's request instantly gave Stazy an image of Jaxon stripped out of those decadent leathers, standing naked beneath a hot shower, the darkness of his hair wet and tousled as rivulets of soapy water ran down his hard and tanned torso—

'Would you like some tea before you go upstairs?' she bit out abruptly, inwardly cursing the way her breasts felt fuller just at her thinking about a naked Jaxon in the shower.

This was ridiculous, damn it! She had never been a sensual being—had certainly never—*ever*!—reacted like this in her life before, let alone found her imagination wandering off into flights of fantasy about a man whose reputation with women was legendary!

'Just the shower and a change of clothes, thanks.'

She nodded. 'I'll have Little take you up to the suite of rooms my grandfather has had prepared for your arrival.'

'Why put the butler to all that trouble when you're already here…?' Jaxon asked huskily.

Stazy stilled, her finger poised over the button that would summon the butler back to the drawing room, before slowly turning to look at Jaxon. The mockery in those assessing grey eyes and the challenging expression on his ruggedly handsome face indicated that he was aware of exactly how much his suggestion had disconcerted her.

Her mouth thinned. 'Fine.'

Jaxon realised this was going to be a long week if the two of them were going to get into a battle of wills over something as small as Stazy showing him up to his suite of rooms!

'I trust you didn't have too much of a problem rear-ranging your departure for Iraq to next week instead of this?' He attempted conversation as the two of them walked up the wide staircase together.

She gave him the briefest of glances from those emerald-green eyes. 'Would it bother you if I had?'

'Honestly? Not really.' He grimaced, only to raise surprised brows as she gave a laugh. A husky laugh that brought a warm glow to those sultry green eyes. A dimple appeared in her left cheek as the parted full-ness of her lips curved into a smile.

Strangely, Jaxon had found himself thinking about those sensuous lips more often than he would have liked these past six weeks. Full and luscious lips that were at odds with the rest of Stazy's buttoned down, no-nonsense appearance… The sort of lips that would be delicious to kiss and taste, and to have kiss and taste him in return…

Something he probably shouldn't think of again when he was already so hard his erection waxs pressing pain-fully against the confines of his leathers!

'Which isn't to say I don't appreciate your having—'

'Oh, don't go and spoil it by apologising, Jaxon.' Stazy still chuckled softly as they reached the top of the stairs and she turned right to walk down the hallway ahead of him. 'If we're to spend any amount of time to-gether then you need to know that I'll appreciate your honesty much more than I would any false charm.'

'My charm is never false,' he snapped irritably.

Stazy turned to quirk a teasing brow. 'Never? Be warned, Jaxon, I'm guilty of having watched film awards on television in the past!'

'Guilty…?'

She snorted. 'Oh, come on, Jaxon—it's all so much glitzy hype, isn't it?'

'I believe the newspapers praised me for the short-ness of my acceptance speech this year,' he drawled.

'I'm not surprised; I thought your co-star was never going to get off the podium!'

'She can be…a little emotional,' Jaxon allowed re-luctantly.

'A little…?' Stazy raised mocking brows. 'She thanked everyone but the man who sweeps the studio floor!'

His eyes narrowed. 'You really can be a—' He broke off with an impatient shake of his head. 'Never mind,' he muttered tersely.

Stazy pushed open the door to the suite of rooms she knew her grandfather had allocated to his guest. The green and cream decor and dark furniture there was more obviously masculine than in some of the other guest suites, as was the adjoining cream and gold bath-room visible through the open doorway. But it was the massive four-poster bed that dominated.

'The sitting room is through here.' She turned away from the intimacy of the bedroom to walk through to the adjoining room with its green carpet and cream sofa. A mahogany desk placed in front of the bay window looked out over the gardens at the back of the house, with the blue of the sea visible above the high wall that surrounded the grounds.

'This is very nice,' Jaxon murmured evenly.

Stazy eyed him derisively. 'You seem a little…tense?'

Those grey eyes narrowed. 'I wonder why!'

She shrugged. 'Can I help it if the much publicised Wilder charm doesn't work on me?'

Jaxon's mouth thinned at the deliberate insult. 'You

shouldn't believe everything you read in trashy magazines!'

Her eyes flashed deeply green. 'I've never read a trashy magazine in my life, thank you very much!'

'Too lowbrow for you?' he taunted.

She drew in a sharp breath. 'My grandfather made it clear to me before he left that he expected me to be polite to a guest in his home during his absence—'

'I hate to be the one to tell you—but so far today you've failed. Miserably!' Jaxon bit out.

Stazy eyed him coolly. 'Being polite doesn't mean I have to be insincere.'

'If you wouldn't mind…?' He began to unzip those body-moulding leathers. 'I would like to take my shower now.' He arched mocking brows.

Stazy had no doubt that Jaxon's challenging attitude now was in return for her earlier scathing comments about 'the much-published Wilder charm'. But as he continued to move that zip further and further down his hard muscled chest she knew it was a challenge she simply didn't have the sophistication—or the experience!—to meet.

'Come downstairs when you're ready and I'll show you the library where we're to work,' she said stiltedly, before turning sharply on her booted heels and hurrying over to the doorway.

Totally aware of the sound of Jaxon's throaty laughter behind her…

'Where do you want to start?'

'I have absolutely no idea.' Jaxon looked down in some dismay at the copious amount of documents and notebooks Geoffrey Bromley had left neatly stacked on the desktop in the library for him to look through.

Jaxon wasn't sure he would be able to get through them all in just the week Stazy had agreed to give him.

The library itself was full of floor to ceiling mahogany bookcases stacked mainly with leather-bound books, although some of the shelves near the door seemed to be full of more modern hardbacks that he might like to explore another time.

Jaxon felt somewhat refreshed after a long cold shower and a change of clothes, and thankfully had succeeded in dissipating the last of his erection as well as washing off the travel dust.

The erection was something—despite their sharp exchange in his suite earlier—that was guaranteed not to stay away for very long if Stazy was going to continue bending over the desk in that provocative way, her denims clearly outlining the perfect curve of her bottom.

'Maybe we should just sort them out year by year today, and start looking through them properly tomorrow?' he prompted tersely.

'Sounds logical.' Stazy nodded.

Jaxon regarded her through narrowed lids. 'And are you big on logic?'

She looked irritated by the implied criticism. 'I've always found it's the best way to approach most situations, yes.'

'Hmm.' He nodded. 'The problem with logic is that it leaves no room for emotion.'

'Which is precisely the point,' Stazy reasoned shortly.

No doubt—but Jaxon didn't work that way. 'Are these Anastasia's diaries?' He ran awed fingers lightly over a pile of a dozen small notebooks.

'They certainly look like them, yes…' Stazy frowned down at them as if they were a bomb about to go off.

He glanced up as he sensed her tension. 'You didn't know there were diaries?'

She gave a pained wince. 'No.'

Jaxon breathed deeply. 'Stazy, as much as you may choose not to think so, I *do* appreciate that none of this can be easy for you—'

Those green eyes flashed in warning. 'I doubt you have any idea how much I hate doing this!'

'Obviously Anastasia was your grandmother, and you only knew her during her latter years, but—'

'But even then she would still have known exactly how to deal with someone like *you*!' Stazy assured him dismissively. Even that red-gold hair seemed to crackle with her repressed anger.

'Like me?' he said softly.

'You know exactly what I mean!'

'I do,' he acknowledged, with that same deceptive mildness. 'I'd just like to hear you say it,' he added challengingly.

She glared her frustration. 'Jaxon, you've known from the first that nothing is going to make me like you *or* your damned film!'

'Nothing...?'

Stazy stilled as she looked up at him guardedly. The darkness of that overlong hair was still damp and slightly tousled from his shower. His jaw was freshly shaven, and he had changed out of the black leathers into a tight-fitting white short-sleeved tee shirt that revealed the tanned strength of his arms and black denims that rested low down on the leanness of his waist.

He looked, in fact, every inch Jaxon Wilder—sex symbol of both the big and little screen. A stark reminder—if Stazy had needed one—of just how little it actually mattered to this man whether or not she liked or approved of him and what he was doing.

Her chin rose determinedly. 'I'm sorry to disappoint you, Jaxon, but I have absolutely no interest in... in providing you with a—a romantic diversion to help while away your leisure time during your week-long stay here,' she assured him derisively.

'What on earth makes you think I would be in the least interested in having you as "a romantic diversion"—now or at any other time...?' His expression was amused as he leant back against the desk and looked down at her with mocking grey eyes, his arms folded across the powerful width of his chest, revealing the bulge of muscle at the tops of his tanned arms.

Stazy's cheeks heated with embarrassed colour at this deliberate set-down. What on earth had she been thinking? Of *course* Jaxon's challenge hadn't been hinting he was in the least interested in her in a personal way!

'But just to set my mind at ease, if things *should* go that way between us I'd be interested to know whether or not you're involved with someone at the moment...?'

When had Jaxon moved so that he now stood only inches away from her? Stazy wondered warily. He was pinning her as he looked down at her with piercing grey eyes.

She moistened her lips with the tip of her tongue. 'I don't see what that has to do with anything...'

'Humour me, hmm?' he encouraged gruffly.

The more immediate problem for Stazy—the whole root of the problem between the two of them—was that from their first meeting she had realised his magnetism was such that she wanted to do so much more than humour this man!

It was totally illogical. Ridiculous. Not only that, but it went totally against everything she had said and thought about this man!

And yet at this moment she literally *ached* to curve her body into his as she ran her hands lightly up the warmth of that muscled chest, over the broad expanse of his shoulders, before allowing her fingers to become entangled in the heavy thickness of that overlong dark hair to pull his head down and have those sensually chiselled lips claim hers...

This wasn't just ridiculous—it was dangerous!

And so completely out of character that Stazy barely recognised herself. Damn it, she didn't even *want* to recognise herself as this woman who couldn't seem to stop fantasising about the two of them in one clinch or another!

She had taken precisely two lovers in her twenty-nine years. The first had been one of her university lecturers, twenty years her senior, on a single night ten years ago. The second one had been a man on a summer dig in Tunisia four years ago—a man who had a wife and children back home in England. Admittedly that was something Stazy had only learnt *after* spending the night with him, when his wife had telephoned to inform him that one of his three children was in hospital and he was needed back home immediately!

Neither of those experiences had resulted in Stazy feeling any warmth or pleasure in the act, let alone having an orgasm. They certainly hadn't prepared her for the seductively lethal charm and good looks of Jaxon Wilder!

She stepped back abruptly. 'As it happens I'm not involved with anyone at the moment. Nor do I wish to be,' she added with cold dismissal.

It was a coldness so at odds with the quickened rise and fall of her breasts, the deepening in colour of those sultry green eyes and the soft swelling of poutingly moist lips, that Jaxon wanted nothing more than to take Stazy in his arms and prove her wrong!

That need hovered in the air between them for several long, tense seconds.

Stazy's chin rose as she deliberately tilted her head back in order to meet his gaze.

Did she have any idea how tempted Jaxon was by that challenge? Of how he wanted nothing more at that moment than to pull her into his arms and kiss the hell out of her?

Stazy was a beautiful woman in her late twenties, and as such she had to be aware of exactly what she was doing. Which begged the question—did she actually *want* him to kiss the hell out of her…?

CHAPTER FOUR

STAZY took a step back as she saw the look of sexual interest that had entered Jaxon's narrowed eyes. 'Perhaps you would like to concentrate on the papers and I'll sort out the diaries?' To her dismay she sounded slightly breathless, and Jaxon was still standing close enough that she was aware of the heat of his body and the tantalising smell of his aftershave.

'Fine,' he agreed huskily, that smoky-grey gaze unblinking.

She continued to eye him warily, very aware that something—she wasn't quite sure what—hung in the balance in these tension filled minutes. Something deep and almost primal. Something so nerve-tinglingly huge that Stazy feared it threatened to tear down the structured life of academia that she had so carefully surrounded herself with these past eleven years!

Jaxon felt as if he could have reached out and touched the sudden and obvious panic that spiked through Stazy as her eyes widened and the slenderness of her body trembled. The very air between them seemed to shimmer with that same emotion.

The question was *why*? What was so wrong with a man finding Stazy attractive enough to want to kiss her? Maybe even make love to her?

Had she been hurt in the past to the extent that it had made her wary of all men? Or did she only feel that wariness where Jaxon was concerned? She had certainly seemed to imply as much earlier!

Admittedly the newspapers had seemed to take great delight in photographing him with the beautiful actresses he'd been involved with during the past ten years; but in reality they really hadn't been that numerous—and a lot of the photographs that had appeared had actually been publicity shots, usually for the film he was currently working on.

Even so, he didn't feel that was any reason for Stazy to look at him in that wary and suspicious way. Almost as if she feared that at any moment he might rip her clothes off before throwing her across the desk and having his wicked way with her!

It was an idea that might merit further investigation, but certainly wasn't something Jaxon thought was likely to happen in the next few minutes!

He eased the tension from his shoulders. 'Shall we make a start then…?'

'Why not?' Stazy felt as if she were emerging from a dream as she forced herself to reply with the same lightness of tone, before ignoring him completely to concentrate all her attention on the piles of papers.

On the surface, at least. Inwardly, it was a different matter!

What had happened just now?

Had *anything* happened…?

Maybe she had just imagined the physical tension that had seemed to crackle briefly in the air between Jaxon and herself? Or—worse—maybe that physical awareness had only been on her side?

No, Stazy was sure it hadn't been. But, as she had

assured him earlier, she certainly knew better than to take seriously any emotional or physical games a man as experienced as Jaxon might decide to play. He was only here for a week, and then he would depart to commence making his pirate film, at which time he would probably forget Dr Stazy Bromley even existed.

As long as she kept reminding herself of that fact she should escape from their week's confinement together unscathed…

'Geoffrey seemed more than a little…evasive as to his reason for the need for extra security when I spoke to him on the telephone earlier…?' Jaxon looked across the dinner table at Stazy. The butler had served them their first course of prawns with avocado before once again leaving them alone together in the small and sun-lit family dining room.

Stazy looked extremely beautiful this evening, having changed into a knee-length red sheath of a dress that should have clashed with that red-gold hair and yet instead somehow managed to add vibrancy to the unusual colour. Her legs were long and shapely in high-heeled red sandals, and her sun-kissed face was once again bare of make-up except for a red gloss on the fullness of her lips. A light dusting of endearing freckles was visible across the bridge of her tiny nose.

It had only taken one look at her when they'd met up in the drawing room before dinner for Jaxon to once again become aroused, quickly bringing him to the conclusion that suffering a whole week of this torment might just be the death of him.

'I did try to warn you that until Gramps has something he thinks we should know he'll play whatever this is pretty close to his chest,' Stazy answered unsympathetically.

Jaxon arched dark brows as she continued to eat her prawns and avocado. 'You seem to be taking it all very calmly?' It 'all' included those security guards at the main gates, as well as half a dozen more he had seen patrolling the grounds when he'd looked out of his bedroom window earlier—several of them accompanied by dogs.

She shrugged slender shoulders. 'I lived here with Granny and Gramps for almost ten years.'

'And you've had other security scares in the past?'

'Once or twice, yes,' Stazy said lightly.

'But—'

'Jaxon, if you're that worried about it you always have the option of leaving,' she reasoned softly.

Great—now she'd managed to make him sound like a complete wuss! 'I'm happy where I am, thanks,' he dismissed—or at least he would be if he didn't feel so on edge about his constant state of arousal whenever he was in Stazy's company!

Admittedly Stazy was beautiful, but she was nowhere near as beautiful as some of the women Jaxon had been involved with in the past. Nor did she make any attempt to hide her distrust of him. In fact the opposite.

Which was perhaps half the attraction…?

Maybe—although somehow Jaxon doubted it. Stazy was like no other woman he had ever met. For one thing she didn't even seem aware of her own beauty. Add that to her obvious intelligence and it was a pretty potent mix.

Jaxon had never been attracted to a woman simply on her looks alone, and he liked to be able to talk to a woman out of bed as well as make love with her in it. Stazy Bromley obviously ticked all the boxes as far as his raging libido was concerned.

Stazy wasn't sure she particularly cared for the way in which Jaxon was looking at her from between those hooded lids—almost as if he were thinking of eating *her* for his dinner rather than the food on his plate!

She had deliberately put on her favourite red dress this evening, in order to give herself the boost in confidence she had felt she lacked earlier. After those tension-filled minutes in her grandfather's library she had felt in need of all the armour she could get where Jaxon Wilder was concerned, and feeling confident about her own appearance was definitely a good place to start.

Or at least it would have been if the moment she'd seen him again she hadn't been so completely aware of how dangerously attractive Jaxon looked this evening, in a loose white silk shirt and those black denims that fitted snugly to the leanness of his muscled thighs and long, long legs…

His shirt was unbuttoned at his throat to reveal the beginnings of a dusting of dark hair that no doubt covered most of his chest. And lower. That 'lower' being exactly where Stazy had forced her thoughts to stop earlier today. Unfortunately she didn't seem to be having the same success this evening!

This just wasn't *her*, damn it. Those two attempts at taking a lover had not only proved completely unsatisfactory but had also firmly put an end to any illusions she might have had where she and men were concerned. She certainly didn't indulge in erotic fantasies about movie stars—or any other man, come to that!—and the sooner her grandfather returned from London and put a stop to this cosy intimacy for two the better!

'So...' Jaxon waited until the butler had been in to clear away their used plates before leaning forward. 'Have I told you how lovely you're looking this evening...?'

That air of intimacy between them became even cosier—in fact the temperature in the room seemed to go up several degrees! 'No, you haven't—and I would prefer that you didn't do so now, either,' Stazy bit out determinedly.

He raised dark brows. 'I thought you asked me for honesty earlier...?'

'Not that sort of honesty!' Her eyes flashed a deep disapproving green. 'We're work colleagues, Jaxon, and work colleagues do not comment on each other's appearance if they are to maintain a proper working relationship.'

'You sound as if you're speaking from experience...?'

Colour warmed her cheeks. 'Perhaps.'

'Feel like telling me about it...?'

Her mouth firmed. 'No.'

Pity, because Jaxon would have liked to know more—a lot more!—about Stazy's personal life. 'Most of the actresses I've worked with would be insulted if I didn't mention their appearance at least once a day.'

Stazy shot him an impatient frown. 'Well, I assure you in my case it isn't necessary. Or appreciated.'

He smiled ruefully. 'I thought all women liked to receive compliments?'

'I would rather be complimented on my academic ability than the way I look,' she stated primly.

Jaxon might have been more convinced of that if Stazy's hand hadn't trembled slightly as she picked up her glass and took a sip of the red wine. 'That's a little difficult for me to do when I know next to noth-ing about your academic ability—other than you're obviously good at what you do—but I can clearly see how beautiful you look in that red dress.'

Those green eyes darkened. 'We aren't out on a date, Jaxon, and no amount of compliments from you is going to result in the two of us ending up in bed together at the end of the evening, either— Damn, damn, *damn*!' she muttered, with an accusing glare in his direction as the butler returned to the dining room just in time to hear that last outburst.

Jaxon barely managed to keep his humour in check as Stazy studiously avoided so much as looking at him again as Little hastily served their food before beating an even hastier retreat. 'Guess what the gossip in the kitchen is going to be about later this evening...' he murmured ruefully.

'This isn't funny, Jaxon,' she bit out agitatedly. 'Little has worked for my grandfather for years. I've known him all my life. And now he's going to think that I—that we—' She broke off with a disbelieving shake of her head.

'Oh, cheer up, Stazy.' Jaxon smiled unconcernedly. 'Look on the bright side—at least I now know where I stand in regard to the possibility of sharing your bed tonight. With any luck, after hearing your last remark, Little will decide to put lighted candles on the dinner table for us tomorrow evening, in an attempt to heat up the romance!'

Much as she hated to admit it, Stazy knew she didn't need any 'heating up' where this man was concerned! And considering it was now July, and the evenings stayed light until after ten o'clock at night, she didn't think there was much chance of any candles appearing on the dinner table—tomorrow night or any other. In fact it was still so light at the moment that the curtains hadn't even been drawn over the floor-to-ceiling windows yet, and the view of a beautiful sunset was certainly adding to the air of romance.

Whatever cutting reply Stazy might have wanted to make to Jaxon's suggestion was delayed as Little returned with a laden tray, his face completely expressionless as he served their main course without meeting the gaze of either one of them before quietly departing again.

'You're enjoying yourself, aren't you?' Stazy eyed Jaxon impatiently as he grinned across the table at her.

Jaxon chuckled softly. 'So would you be if you would just lighten up a little. Oh, come on, Stazy—just think about it for a minute and then admit it *was* funny,' he cajoled irritably as she continued to frown.

'I'll admit no such thing! You—'

'Ever heard the saying about the lady protesting too much...?' He raised mocking brows. 'I've been told that when a lady does that, it usually means she wants you to do the opposite of what she's saying.'

'Whoever told you that was an idiot!' She gave an impatient shake of her head. 'And if you weren't my grandfather's guest I would ask you to leave!'

'Pity about that, isn't it?' he murmured dryly.

Stazy threw her napkin down on the tabletop before standing up and moving away from the table. 'If you will excuse me—'

'No.'

She stilled. 'What do you mean, no?'

'Exactly what I said—no.' The humour had gone from Jaxon's voice and expression, and there was a dark scowl on his brow as he threw down his own napkin before standing up to move purposefully around the table towards her.

Stazy raised a protesting hand even as she instinctively took a step backwards—only to find herself trapped between a looming Jaxon in front of her and a glass cabinet containing china ornaments behind her. 'Stop this right now, Jaxon—'

'Believe me, I haven't even started yet,' he growled, a nerve pulsing in his tightly clenched jaw as he towered over her. 'In fact I think maybe we should just get this over with and then maybe we can move on!' he muttered impatiently.

Stazy looked up at him with startled eyes. 'Get what over with…?'

He gave a shake of his head and lifted his arms to place them either side of her head so that his hands rested on the doors of cabinet behind her, his body almost, but not quite, touching hers. 'For some reason you seem to have decided that at some time during my stay here I'm going to try and seduce you into my bed, so I thought we might as well make a start!'

'You—' Stazy's protest came to an abrupt end as she realised that lifting her hands and placing them against Jaxon's chest, with the intention of pushing him away from her, had been a bad idea. A *very* bad idea…

Her hands lingered. His chest felt very warm to her touch through the soft material of his shirt—like steel encased in velvet as his muscles flexed beneath her fingers. The smell of his cologne—cinnamon and sandalwood—combined with hot, hot male was almost overwhelming to the senses.

Almost?

Stazy ceased to breathe at all as she stared up at Jaxon with wide, apprehensive eyes. Was he right? *Had* she been 'protesting too much'? When in reality she had been longing for this to happen?

God, yes…!

Much as it pained her to admit it, Stazy knew she had thought about Jaxon far too often for comfort in the last six weeks. Damn it, she had even fantasised earlier about what it would be like to be naked with Jaxon, making love with him…

But wanting something and getting it weren't the same things, were they? For instance she had wanted an expensive microscope when she was ten years old—had been convinced at the time that she intended to be a medical doctor when she was older. Her parents had bought her a less expensive microscope, equally convinced that it was just a fad she was going through, with the promise of buying her the more expensive microscope one day if she ever *did* become a doctor.

Maybe not the best analogy, but Stazy no more needed Jaxon in her bed now than she had really needed that very expensive microscope nineteen years ago.

In other words, allowing Jaxon Wilder to kiss her would be an extravagance her emotions just didn't want or need!

Stazy liked her life ordered. Structured. Safe!

Most of all safe…

She had learnt at a very young age that caring for someone, loving them, needing a special someone in your life, was a guarantee of pain in the future when that person either left or—worse—died. As her parents had died. As Granny had died. As her grandfather, now in his nineties, and with that heart attack only a few months ago behind him, would eventually die.

Stazy didn't want to care about anyone else, to need

anyone else—couldn't cope with any more losses in her life.

'Don't do that!' Jaxon groaned huskily.

She raised startled lids. 'Do what?'

'Lick your lips.' The darkness of his gaze became riveted on the moistness of those lips as Stazy ran her tongue nervously between them. 'I've been wanting to do exactly the same thing since the moment we first met,' Jaxon admitted gruffly.

Her eyes were wide. 'You have…?'

He rested his forehead against hers, his breath a warm caress across her already heated cheeks. 'You have the sexiest mouth I've ever seen…'

She gave a choked laugh. 'I thought it was universally acknowledged that that was Angelina Jolie?'

'Until six weeks ago I thought so too.' Jaxon nodded.

He had fantasised about Stazy's mouth these past six weeks. Imagined all the things she could do to him with those deliciously full and pouting lips. Grown hard with need just thinking of that plump fullness against his flesh, kissing him, tasting him. As he now longed to taste her…

'I'm going to kiss you now, Stazy,' Jaxon warned harshly.

'Jaxon, no…!' she groaned in protest.

'Jaxon, yes!' he contradicted firmly, before lowering his head and capturing those full and succulent lips with his own, groaning low in his throat as he found she felt and tasted as good as he had imagined she would!

If Jaxon's mouth had been demanding or rough against hers then Stazy believed she might have been able to resist him. She *hoped* she would have been able to resist him! As it was he kissed her with gentle exploration, sipping, tasting, as his mouth moved over and against hers with a slow languor that was torture to the senses. Taste as well as touch.

Those chiselled lips were surprisingly soft and warm against her own, his body even hotter as Jaxon lowered himself against her with a low groan, instantly making her aware of the hardness of his arousal pressing against her own aching thighs.

Unbidden, it seemed, her hands glided up his chest and over his shoulders, until her fingers at last became entangled with the overlong thickness of that silky dark hair.

He pulled back slightly, and Stazy at once felt bereft without the heat of those exploring lips against her own.

'Say so now if you want me to stop…'

'No…' She was the one to initiate the kiss this time, as she moved up onto her tiptoes, her lips parting to deepen the kiss rather than end it as she held him to her.

It was all the invitation Jaxon needed. He pressed himself firmly against the warm softness of her body as his hands moved to cup either side of her face so that he could explore that delicious mouth more deeply, tongue dipping between her parted lips to enter and explore the moist and inviting heat beneath.

Her taste—warmth and the sweetness of honey, and something indefinably feminine—was completely intoxicating. Like pure alcohol shooting through Jaxon's bloodstream, it threw him off balance, ripping away any awareness of anything other than the taste and feel of Stazy's mouth against his and her warm and luscious body beneath him.

He could only *feel* as Stazy wrapped her arms more tightly about his shoulders and arched her body up and into his, her soft breasts against the hardness of his chest, the heat of her thighs against the hot throb of his arousal. His hands moved down to her waist before sliding around to cup the twin orbs of her bottom to pull her up closer to him.

Jaxon kissed her hungrily, his arousal a fierce throb as Stazy returned the hunger of that kiss, lips hot and demanding, tongues duelling, bodies clamouring for even closer contact.

As Stazy had expected—feared—the tight control she usually exerted over her emotions had departed the moment Jaxon began to kiss her. Her nipples had grown hard and achingly sensitised, and the heat from their kisses was moving between her thighs—a feeling she hadn't experienced even when fully making love with those two men in her past.

She didn't want Jaxon ever to stop. Every achingly aroused inch of her cried out for more. One of his hands moved to cup the fullness of her breast, sending hot rivulets of pleasure coursing through her as his thumb grazed across the aching nipple. Stazy pressed into the heat of his hand, wanting more, needing more, and Jaxon lifted her completely off the floor to wrap her legs about his waist.

She no longer cared that they were in her grandfather's family dining room, or that Little could walk back into the room at any moment to remove their dinner plates.

All she was aware of was Jaxon—the heat of his arousal pressing into her softness, the pleasure that curled and grew inside her as he squeezed her nipple between thumb and finger, just enough to increase her pleasure but not enough to cause her pain, the hardness of him sending that same pleasure coursing through her.

She whimpered in protest as Jaxon broke the kiss, that protest turning to a low and aching moan of pleasure as his mouth moved down the length of her throat, his tongue a hot rasp against her skin as he tasted every hot inch of her from the sensitivity of her earlobe to the exposed hollow where her neck and shoulder met. And all the time his thighs continued that slow and torturous thrust against her.

Stazy still felt as if she were poised on the very edge of a precipice, but no longer cared if she fell over the edge. She wanted this. Wanted Jaxon. He felt so good, so very, very good, that she never wanted this to end…

Jaxon pulled back with a groan, his forehead slightly damp as it rested against hers. 'Lord knows I don't want us to stop, but Little is sure to come back in a few minutes…'

Stazy stared up at him blankly for several seconds, and then her face paled, her eyes widening with dismay as she took in the full import of what had just happened. 'Oh-my-God…!' Her expression was stricken as she struggled to put her feet back onto the floor, her face averted as she pulled out of Jaxon's arms to hastily straighten and pull her dress back down over the silkiness of her thighs.

'Stazy—'

'I think it's best if you don't touch me again, Jaxon,' she warned shakily, even as Jaxon would have done exactly that.

His arms dropped back to his sides as he saw the bewilderment in her eyes. His tone was reasoning. 'Stazy, what happened just now was perfectly normal—'

'It may be "normal" for you, Jaxon, but it certainly isn't normal for me!' she assured tremulously.

'Damn it, I *asked* you if you wanted me to stop!'

'I know…!' she groaned. 'I just— This must never

happen again, Jaxon.' She looked up at him with tear-wet eyes.

'Why not...?'

'It just can't,' she bit out determinedly.

'That isn't a reason—'

'I'm afraid it's the only one you're going to get at the moment,' she confirmed huskily, giving him one last pleading look before turning to hurry across the room to wrench open the door, closing it firmly behind her several seconds later.

Leaving Jaxon in absolutely no doubt that the passionately hot Stazy—the woman he had held in his arms only minutes ago—would be firmly buried beneath cool and analytical Dr Anastasia Bromley by the time the two of them met again...

CHAPTER FIVE

'IF YOU had let me know you were going out riding earlier this morning then I would have come with you, rather than just sat and watched you out of the window as I ate my breakfast...'

Stazy's gaze was cool when she glanced across at Jaxon as he entered the library the following morning. 'To have invited you to accompany me would have defeated the whole object.' Having to accept one of her grandfather's security guards accompanying her, and in doing so severely curtailing where she rode, had been bad enough, without having Jaxon trailing along as well!

After last night he was the last person she had wanted to be with when she'd got up this morning!

Neither of her two experiences had prepared her in the least for the heat, the total wildness, of being in Jaxon's arms the previous evening.

It had been totally out of control. *She* had been out of control!

Her two sexual experiences had been far from satisfactory, and yet she had almost gone over the edge just from having her legs wrapped around Jaxon's waist while he thrust against the silky barrier of her panties!

Having escaped to her bedroom the previous

evening, Stazy had relived every wild and wanton moment of being in Jaxon's arms. The thrumming excitement. The arousal. And—oh, God!—the pleasure! She had trembled from the force of that pleasure, the sensitive ache still between her thighs, her breasts feeling full and sensitised.

She had been so aroused that she dreaded to think what might have happened if Jaxon hadn't called a halt to their lovemaking. Would Jaxon have stripped off her clothes? Worse, would she have ripped off her own clothes? And would he have made love to her on the carpeted floor, perhaps? Or maybe he would have just ripped her panties aside and taken her against the cabinet? Having either of those two things happen would have been not only unacceptable but totally beyond Stazy's previous experience.

'Am I wrong in sensing the implication that you much preferred to go out riding rather than having to sit and eat breakfast with me…?' Jaxon prompted dryly.

She looked across at him. 'Is that what I implied…?'

He eyed her frustratedly. Knowing that beneath Stazy's exterior of cool logic was a woman as passionate as the fiery red-gold of her hair, a woman who had become liquid flame in his arms as she absorbed— consumed!—the blazing demand of his desire before giving it back in equal measure didn't help to ease that frustration in the slightest.

'Besides which,' she continued briskly, 'I was up at six, as usual, and breakfasted not long after.'

Jaxon closed the door behind him before strolling over to sit on the edge of the table where Stazy sat. 'I'll have to remember that you're an early riser if I ever want the two of us to breakfast together.'

Stazy could think of only one circumstance under

which that might be applicable—and it was a circumstance she had no intention of allowing to happen! That didn't mean to say she wasn't completely aware of Jaxon's muscled thigh only inches away from her where he perched on the edge of the table...

He looked disgustingly fit and healthy this morning for a man who had flown over from the States only yesterday: the sharp angles of his face were healthily tanned, that overlong dark hair was slightly damp from the shower, his tee shirt—black today—fitted snugly over his muscled chest and the tops of his arms, and faded denims outlined the leanness of his waist and those long legs. There was only a slightly bruised look beneath those intelligent grey eyes to indicate that Jaxon suffered any lingering jet lag.

'I shouldn't bother for the short amount of time you'll be here,' she advised dryly.

He gave a relaxed smile. 'Oh, it's no bother, Stazy,' he assured her huskily.

She shifted restlessly. 'Considering your time here is limited, shouldn't we get started...?'

Jaxon didn't need any reminding that he now had only six days left in which to do his research. Just as he didn't need to be told that it was Stazy's intention to keep her distance from him for those same six days...

There had been a few moments of awkwardness the previous evening, when he'd told Little that Stazy wasn't feeling well enough to finish her meal and had gone upstairs to her bedroom. The knowing look in the older man's eyes, before he'd quietly cleared away her place setting had been indicative of his scepticism at that explanation. But, being the polite English butler that he was, Little hadn't questioned the explanation—or Jaxon's claim that *he* didn't want any more to eat either.

Food, at least...

Jaxon's appetite for finishing what he and Stazy had started had been a different matter entirely!

Once upstairs, despite feeling exhausted, he had paced the sitting room of his suite for hours as he thought of Stazy's fiery response to his kisses, his shaft continuing to throb and ache as he remembered having her legs wrapped about his waist, the moist heat between her thighs as he pressed against her.

A virtually sleepless night later he only had to look at her again this morning to recall the wildness of their shared passion. The fact that her appearance was every inch the prim and cold Dr Anastasia Bromley again today—hair pulled back and plaited down the length of her spine, green blouse loose rather than fitted over tailored black trousers, and flat no-nonsense shoes—in no way dampened the eroticism of last night's memories.

In fact the opposite; if anything, that air of cool practicality just made Jaxon want to kiss her until he once again held that responsive woman in his arms!

'Fine.' He straightened abruptly before taking the seat opposite hers and concentrating on the pile of papers Geoffrey Bromley had left for him to look through.

That was not to say he wasn't completely aware of Stazy as she sat opposite him. He could smell her perfume—a light floral and her own warm femininity—and the sunlight streaming through the window was turning her hair to living flame. A flame Jaxon wanted to wrap about his fingers as he once again took those full and pouting lips beneath his own...

'Have you heard from Geoffrey this morning?' he prompted gruffly after several minutes of torturous silence—minutes during which he was too aware of Stazy to be able to absorb a single thing he had read.

She shook her head. 'As I've already told you, my grandfather has become a law unto himself since Granny died.'

Jaxon sat back in his chair. 'And before that...?'

Her gaze instantly became guarded. 'What exactly is it you want to know, Jaxon?'

He shrugged. 'All my own research so far gives the impression their long marriage was a happy one.'

'"So far"?'

Discussing Stazy's grandparents with her had all the enjoyment of walking over hot coals: one wrong step and he was likely to get seriously burned! 'You know, we're going to get along much better if you don't keep reading criticism into every statement I make.' He sighed.

It wasn't in Stazy's immediate or long term plans to 'get along' with Jaxon. In fact, after her uncharacteristic behaviour last night, she just wanted this whole thing to be over and done with. 'Sorry,' she bit out abruptly.

'So?'

'So, yes, their marriage was a long and happy one,' she confirmed evenly. 'Not joined at the hip,' she added with a frown. 'They were both much too independent in nature for that. But emotionally close. Always.'

'That's good.' Jaxon nodded, making notes in the pad he had brought downstairs with him.

Stazy regarded him curiously. 'You mentioned your own parents when you were here last...are they happily married?'

'Oh, yes.' An affectionate smile curved Jaxon's lips as he looked up. 'My brother, too. One big happy family, in fact, and all still living in Cambridgeshire. I'm the only one in the family to have left the area and avoided the matrimonial noose,' he added dryly.

Stazy doubted that he was in any hurry to marry, considering the amount of women reputedly queuing up to share the bed of Jaxon Wilder. Something she had been guilty of herself the previous evening…!

'I don't suppose your lifestyle is in any way…conducive to a permanent relationship,' she dismissed coolly.

Jaxon studied her through narrowed lids. 'Any more than your own is. An archaeologist who travels around the world on digs every chance she gets…' he added with a shrug as she looked at him enquiringly.

She smiled tightly. 'That's one of the benefits of being unattached, yes.'

'And what do you consider the other advantages to be?' he prompted curiously.

She gave a lightly dismissive laugh. 'The same as yours, I expect. Mostly the freedom to do exactly as I wish *when* I wish.'

'And the drawbacks…?'

A frown creased the creaminess of her brow. 'I wasn't aware there were any…'

'No…?'

'No.'

He raised dark brows. 'How about no one to come home to at the end of the day? To talk to and be with? To share a meal with? To go to bed with?' He smiled ruefully. 'I suppose it can all be summed up in one word—loneliness.'

Was she ever lonely? Stazy wondered. Probably. No—definitely. And for the reasons Jaxon had just stated. At the end of a long day of teaching she always returned home to her empty apartment, prepared and ate her meal alone, more often than not spending the evening alone, before sleeping alone.

That was exactly how she preferred it! Not just preferred it, but had deliberately arranged her life so it would be that way. Apart from her grandfather, she didn't want or need anyone in her life on a permanent basis. Didn't want or need the heartache of one day losing them—to death or otherwise.

She eyed Jaxon teasingly. 'I find it difficult to believe that you ever need be lonely, Jaxon!'

He gave a tight smile. 'Never heard the saying "feeling alone in a crowd"?'

'And that describes you?'

'Sometimes, yes.'

'I somehow can't see that…' she dismissed.

'Being an actor isn't all attending glitzy parties and awards ceremonies, you know.'

'Let's not forget you get to escort beautiful actresses to both!' she teased.

'No, let's not forget that,' he conceded dryly.

'And you get to go to all those wonderful places on location too—all expenses paid!'

Jaxon smiled wryly. 'Oh, yes. I remember what a wonderful time I had being in snake and crocodile infested waters for days at a time during the making of *Contract with Death*!'

Her eyes widened. 'I'd assumed you had a double for those parts of the film…'

And from the little Stazy had said during that first meeting six weeks ago Jaxon had assumed *she* was far too much the academic to have ever bothered to see a single one of his films! 'I don't use doubles any more than I do hair extensions.'

'You must be a nightmare for film studios to insure.'

'No doubt.'

'What about the flying in *Blue Skies*…?'

He shrugged. 'I went to a village in Bedfordshire where they have a museum of old working planes and learnt to fly a Spitfire.'

A grudging respect entered those green eyes. 'That was…dedicated. What about riding the elephant in *Dark Horizon*?'

He grinned. 'Piece of cake!'

'Riding a horse bareback in *Unbridled*?'

He gave her a knowing look. 'A blessed relief after the elephant!'

'Captaining a boat in *To the Depths*?'

So Stazy obviously hadn't seen just one of his films, but several. Although Jaxon was sure that Stazy had absolutely no idea just how much she was revealing by this conversation. 'I used to spend my summers in Great Yarmouth, helping out on my uncle's fishing boat, when I was at university.'

Her eyes widened. 'You attended university?'

Jaxon was enjoying himself. 'Surprised to learn I'm not just a pretty face, after all?'

If Stazy was being honest? Yes, she *was* surprised. 'What subject did you take?'

He quirked a teasing brow. 'Are you sure you really want me to answer that?'

She felt a sinking sensation in her chest. 'Archaeology?'

'History and archaeology.'

She winced. 'You have a degree in history and archaeology?'

He gave a grin. 'First-class Masters.'

'With what aim in mind…?'

He shrugged. 'I seriously thought about teaching before I was bitten by the acting bug.'

'Why didn't you tell me that before?' Before she'd made a fool of herself and treated him as if he were just another empty-headed movie star. That, in retrospect, had not only been insulting but presumptuous...

Jaxon shrugged wide shoulders. 'You didn't ask. Besides which,' he continued lightly, 'you were having far too much fun looking down your nose at a frivolous Hollywood actor for me to want to spoil it for you.'

Because it had been easier to think of Jaxon that way than to acknowledge him as not only being a handsome movie star but also an intelligent and sensitive man. Which he obviously was...

A dangerous combination, in fact!

Stazy straightened briskly. 'Shall we get on?'

In other words: conversation over, Jaxon acknowledged ruefully. But, whether she realised it or not, he had learnt a little more about Stazy this morning; it was a little like extracting teeth, but very slowly he was learning the intricacies that made up the personality of the beautiful and yet somehow vulnerable Stazy Bromley.

And finding himself intrigued and challenged by all of them...

'Time for lunch, I believe...'

Stazy had been so lost in reading one of her grandmother's diaries that she had momentarily forgotten that Jaxon sat across the table from her, let alone noticed the passing of time. Surprisingly, it had been a strangely companionable morning, that earlier awkwardness having dissipated as they both became lost in their individual tasks.

She gave a shake of her head now. 'I rarely bother to eat lunch.'

'Meaning that I shouldn't either?' Jaxon teased.

'Not at all,' she told him briskly. 'I'll just carry on here, if you would like to go and— What are you doing...?' She frowned across at Jaxon as he reached across the table to close the diary she was reading before rising to his feet and holding out his hand to her expectantly.

'Ever heard the saying "all work and no play..."'

Her mouth firmed as she continued to ignore his outstretched hand. 'I've never pretended to be anything other than dull.'

'I don't find you in the least dull, Stazy,' Jaxon murmured softly.

She raised startled eyes. 'You don't?'

'No,' he assured her huskily; having spent the past three hours completely aware of Stazy sitting across the table from him, how could he claim otherwise? She was a woman of contradictions: practical by nature but delicately feminine in her appearance. Her hands alone seemed proof of that contradiction. Her wrists were fragile, her fingers slender and elegant, but they were tipped with practically short and unvarnished nails. He had spent quite a lot of the last three hours looking at Stazy's hands as she turned the pages of the diary she was reading and imagining all the places those slender fingers tipped by those trimmed nails might linger as she caressed him...

'Let's go, Stazy,' he encouraged her now. 'I asked Little earlier if he would provide us with a lunch basket.'

She frowned. 'You expect me to go on a picnic with you?'

'Why not?' Jaxon asked softly.

Probably because Stazy couldn't remember the last time she had done anything as frivolous as eating her lunch *al fresco*—even in one of the many cafés in England that now provided tables for people to eat outside. When she was working she was too busy during the day to eat lunch at all, and when she came here her grandfather preferred formality. Occasionally Granny had organised a picnic down on the beach at the weekends, but that had been years ago, and—

'You think too much, Stazy.' Jaxon, obviously tired of waiting for her to make up her mind, pulled her effortlessly to her feet.

Stazy couldn't think at all when she was standing close to Jaxon like this, totally aware of the heat of his body and the pleasant—*arousing*—smell of the cologne he favoured. 'Aren't we a little old to be going on a picnic, Jaxon?'

'Not in the least,' he dismissed easily. Not waiting to hear any more of her objections, his hand still firmly clasping hers, he pulled her along with him to walk out into the cavernous hallway. 'Ah, Little, just in time.' He smiled warmly at the butler as he appeared from the back of the house with a picnic basket in one hand and a blanket in the other. 'If Mr Bromley calls we'll be back in a couple of hours.'

Jaxon handed Stazy the blanket before taking the picnic basket himself, all the time retaining that firm grasp on Stazy's hand as he kept her at his side. He strode out of the front doorway of the house and down the steps onto the driveway.

The warm and strong hand totally dwarfed Stazy's, and at the same time she was tinglingly aware of that warmth and strength. The same strength that had enabled him to ride an elephant, go bareback on a horse, to handle the controls of a Spitfire and captain a fishing boat, and do all of those other stunts in his films that Stazy had assumed were performed by someone else.

Making Jaxon far less that 'pretty face' image she had previously taken such pleasure in attributing to him...

If she were completely honest with herself Jaxon was so much more than she had wanted him to be before meeting him, and as such had earned—albeit grudgingly!—her respect. It would have been far easier to simply dismiss the pretty-faced Hollywood actor of her imaginings; but the real Jaxon Wilder was nothing at all as Stazy had thought—hoped—he would be. Instead, he had a depth and intelligence she found it impossible to ignore.

Add those things to the way he looked—to the way he had kissed her and made her feel the previous evening—and Stazy was seriously in danger of fighting a losing battle against this unwanted attraction.

That was why it really wasn't a good idea to go on a picnic with him!

He turned to look down at her from beneath hooded lids. 'Beach or woody glade?'

'Neither.' Stazy impatiently pulled her hand free of his. 'I really don't have time for this, Jaxon—'

'Make time.'

She eyed him derisively. 'Did you need to practise that masterful tone or does it just come naturally?'

Jaxon grinned unconcernedly. 'Just getting into character for next week, when I become captain of a pirate ship and need to keep my female captive in line.'

'Seriously?'

The look of total disbelief on Stazy's face was

enough to make him chuckle out loud. 'Seriously.' He grinned. 'That's before I have my wicked way with her about halfway through the movie, of course.'

She winced. 'After which she no doubt keeps *you* in line?'

'I seem to recall I then become her willing slave in the captain's cabin, yes,' Jaxon allowed dryly, enjoying the delicate blush that immediately coloured Stazy's cheeks; for a twenty-nine-year-old woman she was incredibly easy to shock. 'So, Stazy—beach or woody glade?' He returned to their original conversation.

Stazy's thoughts had briefly wandered off to images of herself as Jaxon's captive on his pirate ship, where he swept her up in his arms. Her hair was loose and windswept, and she was wearing a green velvet gown that revealed more than it covered as he lowered his head and his mouth plundered hers.

Just imagining it was enough to cause her body to heat and her nipples to tingle and harden inside her bra as the warm feeling between her thighs returned.

Good grief…!

She gave a self-disgusted shake of her head as she dismissed those images. 'I think you'll find that my grandfather's security guards might have something to say about where we're allowed to go for our picnic.' She grimaced as she recalled how her ride this morning had been decided by one of those attentive guards.

'Let's walk down to the beach and see if anyone tries to stop us.' Once again Jaxon took a firm hold of her hand, before walking towards the back of the house and the pathway down to the beach.

Dragging a reluctant Stazy along with him…

CHAPTER SIX

No one tried to stop them, but Jaxon noted the presence of the two black-clothed men who moved to stand at either end of the coved beach that stretched beyond the walled gardens of Bromley House, positioning themselves so that they faced outwards rather than watching the two of them as he and Stazy spread the blanket on the warmth of the sand.

The sun was shining brightly and a breeze blew lightly off the sea.

'Little seems to have thought of everything,' Jaxon murmured appreciatively as he uncorked a bottle of chilled white wine before pouring it into the two crystal glasses he had unwrapped from tissue paper.

'Years of practice, I expect.' There was a wistful note in Stazy's voice as she knelt on the blanket, arranging the chicken and salad onto plates.

His expression was thoughtful as he sipped his wine. 'You used to come here with your grandparents.' It was a statement rather than a question.

She nodded abruptly. 'And my parents when they were still alive.'

'I hadn't realised that.' He winced. 'Would you rather have gone somewhere else?'

'Not at all,' she dismissed briskly. 'I'm sure you

know me well enough by now, Jaxon, to have realised I have no time for sentimentality,' she added dryly.

No, Jaxon couldn't say he had 'realised' that about her at all. Oh, there was no doubting that Stazy liked to give the impression of brisk practicality rather than warmth and emotion; but even in the short time Jaxon had spent in her company he had come to realise that was exactly what it was—an impression. Even if she hadn't responded to him so passionately—so wildly—the evening before he would still have known that about her. Her defence of her grandparents, everything she said and did in regard to them, revealed that she loved them deeply. And as she had no doubt loved her parents just as deeply…

'Where were you when your parents died…?' He held out the second glass of chilled wine to her.

Her fingers trembled slightly as she took the glass from him. 'At boarding school.' Her throat moved convulsively as she swallowed. 'My father was flying the two of them to Paris to celebrate their twentieth wedding anniversary.'

'Do you know what went wrong…?'

Her eyes were pained as she looked up at him. 'Are you really interested, Jaxon, or are these questions just out of a need for accuracy in your screenplay—'

'I'm really interested,' he cut in firmly, more than a little irritated that she could ask him such a question. Admittedly they had only met at all because of the film he wanted to make about her grandmother, but after their closeness last night he didn't appreciate having Stazy still view his every question with suspicion. 'I've already decided that neither you nor your parents will feature in the film, Stazy.'

She raised red-gold brows. 'Why not?'

Jaxon shook his head. 'There's only so much I can cover in a film that plays for a couple of hours without rushing it, so I've more or less decided to concentrate on the escape of Anastasia's family from Russia, her growing up in England, and then the earlier years of the love story between Anastasia and Geoffrey.'

Her expression softened. 'It really was a love story, wasn't it?'

Again there was that wistful note in Stazy's voice. Jaxon was pretty sure she was completely unaware of it. An unacknowledged yearning, perhaps, for that same enduring love herself...? Yet at the same time Stazy was so determined to give every outward appearance of not needing those softer emotions in her life.

She seemed to recognise and shake off that wistfulness as she answered him with her usual briskness. 'There's no mystery about my parents' deaths, Jaxon. The enquiry found evidence that the plane crashed due to engine failure—possibly after a bird flew into it. One of those one in a million chances that occasionally happen.' She shrugged dismissively.

It *was* a one in a million chance, Jaxon knew, and it had robbed Stazy of her parents and completely shattered her young life. A one in a million chance that had caused her to build barriers about her emotions so that her life—and her heart?—would never suffer such loss and heartache again...

He was pretty sure he was getting close to the reason for Stazy's deliberate air of cold practicality. A coldness and practicality that he had briefly penetrated when the two of them had kissed so passionately the evening before...

He reached out to lightly caress one of her creamy cheeks. 'Not everyone leaves or dies, Stazy—'

He knew he had made a mistake when she instantly flinched away from the tenderness of his fingers, her expression one of red-cheeked indignation as she rose quickly to her feet.

'What on earth do you think you're doing, Jaxon?' She glared down at him, her hands clenched into fists at her sides, her breasts rapidly rising and falling in her agitation. 'Did you really think all you had to do was offer a few platitudes and words of understanding in order for me to tumble willingly into your arms? Or is it that your ego is so big you believe every woman you meet is going to want to fall into bed with you?'

Jaxon drew his breath in sharply at the deliberate insult of her attack, his hand falling back to his side as he rose slowly to his feet to look down at her gloweringly. 'It's usually polite to wait until you're asked!'

'Then I advise you not to put yourself to the trouble where I'm concerned!' she bit out dismissively, two bright spots of angry colour in her cheeks, green eyes glittering furiously as she glared up at him. 'I may have made the mistake of allowing you to kiss me last night, but I can assure you I don't intend to make a habit of it!'

Jaxon gave a frustrated shake of his head. 'You kissed me right back, damn it!'

Stazy knew that! Knew it, and regretted it with every breath in her body. At the same time as she wanted to kiss Jaxon again. To have him kiss her. Again. And again...!

She ached for Jaxon to kiss her. To more than kiss her. Had been wanting, aching for him to kiss her again ever since the two of them had parted the night before. So much so that right now she wanted nothing more than for the two of them to lie down on this blanket

on the sand—regardless of the presence of those two
guards!—and have him make love to her.

That was precisely the reason she wouldn't allow it
to happen!

Jaxon was only staying here at Bromley House for a
week. Just one week. After which time he would leave
to make his pirate movie, before returning to the States
and his life there. It would be madness on Stazy's part
to allow herself to become involved with him even for
that short length of time.

Why would it? The only two relationships she'd
previously had in her life had been with men she had
known were uninterested in a permanent relationship.
Surely making Jaxon the perfect candidate for a brief,
week-long affair…

No, she couldn't do it! She sensed—knew—from the
wildness of her response to him yesterday evening that
Jaxon represented a danger to all those barriers she had
so carefully built about her emotions. So much so that
she knew even a week of being Jaxon's lover would be
six days and twenty-three hours too long…!

'Where are you going?' Jaxon reached out to firmly
grasp Stazy's arm as she would have turned and walked
away.

'Back to the house—'

'In other words, you're running away?' he scorned.
'Again,' he added, those grey eyes taunting.

Just the touch of his fingers about her arm was
enough to rob Stazy of her breath. For her to be completely aware of him. Of his heat. His smell. For her
fingers to itch, actually ache to become entangled in
the long length of his hair as his lips, that sensuously
sculptured mouth, claimed hers.

What was it about this man, this man in particular,

that made Stazy yearn to lose herself in his heat? To forget everything and everyone else as she gave in to the rapture of that sensuous mouth, the caresses of his strong and capable hands?

Danger!

To her, Jaxon represented a clear and present danger.

Physically.

Emotionally.

At the same time Stazy knew she had no intention of revealing her weakness by running away from the challenge of his taunt. She pulled her arm free of his steely grasp. 'I happen to be *walking* away, Jaxon, not running. And I'm doing so because I'm becoming bored by the constant need you feel to live up to your less than reputable image!'

The hardness of his cheekbones became clearly defined as his jaw tightened harshly. 'Really?'

'Really,' she echoed challengingly.

Jaxon continued to meet the challenge in those glittering green eyes for several long seconds as he fought an inner battle with himself, knowing the wisest thing he could to do was to let Stazy go, while at the same time wanting to take her in his arms and kiss her into submission. No—not submission; he wanted Stazy to take as much from him as he would be asking of her.

In your dreams, Wilder!

Stazy might have had a brief lapse in control the evening before, but he had no doubt it was that very lapse that made her so determined not to allow him to get close to her again. If he even attempted to kiss her now she would fight him with every part of her. And he didn't want to fight Stazy. He wanted to make love to her...

He also had no doubt that at the first sign of a struggle

between the two of them those two watching bodyguards would decide that Stazy was the one in need of protection. From him…

He stepped back. 'Then I really mustn't continue to bore you any longer, must I?' he drawled dryly.

Stazy looked up at him wordlessly for several seconds, slightly stunned at his sudden capitulation. What had she expected? That Jaxon would ask—plead—for her not to go back to the house just yet? To stay and have lunch with him here instead? That he would ask her for more than just to have lunch with him? If she had thought—hoped for—that then she was obviously going to be disappointed. Jaxon Wilder could have any woman he wanted. He certainly didn't need to waste his time charming someone who continued to claim she wasn't interested.

'Fine,' she bit out tautly. 'Enjoy your lunch.' Her head was held high as she turned and walked away.

Jaxon watched her leave through narrowed lids, knowing that he had allowed Stazy to get to him with those last cutting remarks, and feeling slightly annoyed with himself for allowing her to do so. And, damn it, what 'less than reputable image' was she referring to?

Okay, so over the past ten years or so he'd had his share of relationships with beautiful women. But only two or three in a year. And only ever one at a time. He certainly wasn't involved with anyone at the moment.

He was allowing Stazy's remark to put him on the defensive, when there was nothing for him to feel defensive about!

Jaxon turned slightly as he saw the nearest guard had moved off the headland and was now following Stazy back to the house. His smile became rueful as he watched the second guard leave his position in order to follow behind them, nodding curtly to Jaxon as he passed by several feet away, at the same time letting him know *he* wasn't the one being protected.

Just watching the way the two men moved so stealthily told Jaxon they were attached to one of the Special Forces, and even though neither man carried any visible weapon Jaxon was certain that they were both probably armed.

That knowledge instantly brought back the feelings of unease Jaxon had felt when he had arrived yesterday…

'Ready to call it a day…?'

Stazy had been wary of Jaxon's mood when he'd returned to the house an hour after she had left him so abruptly on the beach, but her worries had proved to be unfounded. Whatever Jaxon felt about that heated exchange, it was hidden beneath a veneer of smooth politeness she found irritating rather than reassuring; either Jaxon had a very forgiving nature, or her remarks had meant so little to him he had totally dismissed them from his mind!

She glanced at the plain gold watch on her wrist now, as she leant against the back of her chair, surprised to see it was almost half past six in the evening.

'Jaxon, I—' She drew in a deep breath before continuing. 'I believe I owe you an apology for some of the things I said to you earlier…'

'You do?' Jaxon raised dark brows as he flexed his shoulder in a stretch after hours of sitting bent over the table, the two of them having only stopped work briefly when Little had brought in a tray of afternoon tea a couple of hours ago.

Stazy had been just as distracted by Jaxon's physical

proximity this afternoon as she had this morning, and now found herself watching the play of muscles beneath his tee shirt as he stretched his arms above his head before standing up. His waist was just as tautly muscled above those powerful thighs and long legs. Damn it, even that five o'clock shadow looked sexy on Jaxon!

And she was once again ogling him like some starstruck groupie, Stazy realised self-disgustedly.

'My grandfather would be…disappointed if he were to learn I had been rude to guest in his home,' she said.

'I'm not about to tell him, Stazy.' Jaxon gave a rueful shake of his head. 'And technically we weren't *in* your grandfather's home at the time.'

'Nevertheless—'

'Just forget about it, okay?' he bit out tautly, no longer quite as relaxed as he had been. 'But, for the record, that disreputable image you keep referring to is greatly overstated!'

Obviously she had been wrong. It hadn't been a case of Jaxon having a forgiving nature *or* her remarks meaning so little to him he had dismissed them at all; Jaxon was just better at hiding his annoyance than most people!

'I only said that because—' She broke off the explanation as she remembered exactly why she had felt defensive enough to make that less than flattering remark earlier. Because she had once again been completely physically aware of Jaxon. Because she had been terrified of her own aching response to that physical awareness, of the danger Jaxon represented to her cool control…

She gave a shake of her head. 'Did you find anything interesting in my grandmother's papers?'

Stazy's attempt at an apology just now had gone a

long way to cementing the fragile truce that had existed between the two of them this afternoon, and in the circumstances Jaxon wasn't sure this was the right time to discuss anything he might or might not have read in Anastasia's private papers.

'A couple of things I'd like to discuss with Geoffrey when I see him next.'

'Such as?'

'It can wait until Geoffrey comes back,' he dismissed.

Stazy's mouth firmed. 'I thought the whole reason for my being here was so that you didn't need to bother my grandfather with any questions…?'

Jaxon gave a rueful smile. 'And I thought the reason you had decided to be here was to make sure I didn't decide to run off with any of any of these private papers!'

'I'm sure the security guards would very much enjoy ensuring you weren't able to do that!' she came back dryly.

'Thanks!' Jaxon grimaced.

She gave him a rueful smile of her own. 'You're welcome!'

That smile transformed the delicacy of her features into something truly beautiful: her eyes glowed deeply green, there was a becoming flush to her cheeks, and her lips were full, curved invitingly over small and even white teeth.

An invitation, if Jaxon should decide to risk taking it up, that would no doubt result in those teeth turning around and biting him.

Now, *there* was a thought guaranteed to ensure he didn't sleep again tonight!

Stazy's smile slowly faded as she saw the flare of

awareness in the sudden intensity of Jaxon's gaze fixed on her parted lips. 'I think I'll go upstairs for a shower before dinner,' she said briskly.

'I'd offer to come and wash your back for you if I didn't already know what your answer would be,' he finished mockingly.

Stazy looked up into that lazily handsome face—warm and caressing grey eyes, those sculptured lips curved into an inviting smile, that sexy stubble on the squareness of his chin—and briefly wished that her answer didn't have to be no. That she really was the sophisticated woman she tried so hard to be—the woman capable of just enjoying the moment by separating the physical from the emotional.

The same woman she had succeeded in being during those other two brief sexual encounters in her past…

But not with Jaxon, it seemed.

Because her reaction to him was frighteningly different…

He quirked one expectant dark brow. 'You seem to be taking a while to think it over…?'

'Not at all.' Stazy shook herself out of that confusion of thoughts. 'I'm just amazed—if not surprised!—at your persistence in continuing to flirt with me.'

He gave an unconcerned shrug. 'It would appear I have something of a reputation to live up to.'

Stazy gave a pained wince. 'I have apologised for that remark.'

'And I've accepted that apology.' He nodded.

'But not forgotten it…?'

No, Jaxon hadn't forgotten it. Or stopped questioning as to the reason why Stazy felt the need to resort to insulting him at all…

Did he make her feel threatened in some way? And,

if so, why? Once again he acknowledged that Stazy Bromley had to be one of the most complex and intriguing women he had ever met. On the outside beautiful, capable and self-contained. But beneath that cool exterior there was a woman of deep vulnerability who used that outer coldness to avoid any situation in which her emotions might become involved. Including physical intimacy. *Especially* physical intimacy!

Not that Jaxon thought for one moment that Stazy was still a virgin. But she would have chosen her lovers carefully. Coolly. Men who were and wished to remain as unemotionally involved as she was.

Had she found enjoyment in those encounters? Had she managed to maintain those barriers about her emotions even during the deepest of physical intimacy?

The cool detachment of her gaze as she looked at him now seemed to indicate those relationships hadn't even touched those barriers, let alone succeeded in breaching them.

As Jaxon so longed to do...

Last night he had briefly seen a different Stazy—a Stazy who had become a living flame in his arms as she met and matched his passion, her fingers entangled in his hair as she wrapped her legs about his waist to meet each slow and pleasurable thrust of his erection against the moist arousal nestled between her thighs.

Jaxon's hands clenched at his sides as he fought against taking her in his arms and kissing her until she once again became that beautiful and intoxicating woman.

'I think I'll go outside for a stroll before dinner.' And

hope that the fresh air would dampen down his renewed arousal!

If not, there was always the coldness of the English Channel he could throw himself into to cool off...!

CHAPTER SEVEN

'I'VE invited an old friend of my grandfather's to join us for dinner this evening,' Stazy informed Jaxon when he came into the drawing room an hour later.

'Really?' He strolled further into the room. He was wearing a black silk shirt unbuttoned at the throat this evening, with black tailored trousers. His hair was once again damp from the shower, the square strength of his chiselled jaw freshly shaven.

Stazy was quickly coming to realise that Jaxon used that noncommittal rejoinder when he was less than pleased with what had been said to him. 'I thought you might be getting a little bored here with just me for company,' she came back lightly as she handed him a glass of the dry martini she now knew he preferred before dinner.

'Did you?' he drawled softly.

She felt the warmth of colour enter her cheeks at his continued lack of enthusiasm. 'Obviously you're used to more sophisticated entertainments—'

'All the more reason for me to enjoy a week of peace and quiet.' Jaxon met her gaze steadily.

'I was only trying to be hospitable—'

'No, Stazy, you weren't,' he cut in mildly.

She stiffened. 'Don't presume to tell me what my motives are, Jaxon.'

'Fine.' He shrugged before strolling across the room to sit down in one of the armchairs, placing his untouched drink down on a side table before resting his elbows on the arms of the chair and steepling his fingers together in front of his chest. 'So who is this "old friend" of your grandfather's?'

Stazy's heart was beating so loudly in her chest she thought Jaxon must be able to hear it all the way across the room. He was right, of course; she hadn't invited Thomas Sullivan to dinner because she had thought Jaxon might be bored with her company—she had invited the other man in the hope he would act as a buffer against this increasing attraction she felt for Jaxon!

For the same reason she was wearing the same plain black shift dress she had worn six weeks ago, when she and Jaxon had first met, with a light peach gloss on her lips and her hair secured in a neat chignon.

She moistened dry lips. 'He and my grandfather were at university together.'

Jaxon raised dark brows. 'That *is* an old friend. And your grandfather's…outside employees are okay with his coming here this evening?'

'I didn't bother to ask them,' she dismissed.

'Then perhaps you should have done.'

Stazy frowned. 'We aren't prisoners here, Jaxon.'

He gave a slight smile. 'Have you tried leaving?'

'Of course not—' Her eyes widened as she broke off abruptly. 'Are you saying that you tried to leave earlier and were prevented from doing so…?'

Jaxon wasn't sure whether Stazy was put out because he might have tried to leave, or because he had been stopped from doing so. Either way, the result was the same: it appeared that for the moment neither of them were going anywhere.

'I had half an hour or so to spare before dinner and thought I would go for a ride—enjoy looking at some of the scenery in the area. I was stopped at the main gate and told very firmly that no one was allowed in or out of Bromley House this evening. Which probably means your grandfather's old friend isn't going to get in either,' he added derisively.

'But that's utterly ridiculous!' She looked totally bewildered as she placed her glass down on a side table before turning towards the door. 'I'll go and speak to one of them now.'

'You do that.' Jaxon nodded. 'And while you're at it maybe you can ask them what that flurry of activity was half an hour or so ago.'

Stazy stopped in her tracks and turned slowly back to face him. 'What flurry of activity?'

He shrugged. 'Extra chatter on the radios, and then about half a dozen more guards arrived fifteen minutes or so later—several of them with more dogs.'

Her cheeks were now the colour of fine pale porcelain. 'I wasn't aware of any of that...'

'No?' Jaxon stood up abruptly, frowning as Stazy instinctively took a step backwards. 'I think you have a much bigger problem here to worry about than me, Stazy,' he said harshly.

She looked even more bewildered. 'I'll telephone my grandfather and ask him what's going on—'

'I already tried that.' A nerve pulsed in Jaxon's clenched jaw. 'I even explained to the woman who answered my call that I was staying here with you at Bromley House at Sir Geoffrey's invitation. It made absolutely no difference. I was still politely but firmly told that Sir Geoffrey wasn't able to come to the telephone at the moment, but that she would pass the message along.'

Stazy gave a slow shake of her head. 'That doesn't sound like my grandfather...'

'I thought so too.' Jaxon nodded tersely. 'So I tried calling him on the mobile number he gave me. It was picked up by an answering service. Needless to say I didn't bother to leave another message— Ah, Little.' He turned to the butler as the other man quietly entered the drawing room. 'Dr Bromley and I were just speculating as to the possible reason for the extra guards in the grounds...'

To his credit, the older man's expression remained outwardly unchanged by the question. But years of acting, of studying the nuances of expression on people's faces, of knowing that even the slightest twitch of an eyebrow could have meaning, had resulted in Jaxon being much more attuned than most to people's emotions.

Even so, if he hadn't actually been looking straight at the older man he might have missed the slight hardening of his brown eyes before that emotion was neatly concealed by the lowering of hooded lids. Leaving Jaxon to speculate whether that small slip might mean that Little was more than just a butler.

'It seems that several teenagers were apprehended earlier today, trying to climb over the walls of the estate with the idea of throwing a party down on the beach,' Little dismissed smoothly.

'Really?' Jaxon drawled dryly.

'Yes,' the older man confirmed abruptly, before turning to Stazy. 'Dinner is ready to be served, Miss Stazy. Mr Sullivan telephoned a few minutes ago to extend his apologies. Due to a slight indisposition he is unable to join the two of you for dinner this evening after all.'

'What a surprise!' Jaxon looked across at Stazy knowingly.

To say *she* was surprised by all of this was putting it mildly. In fact she had been more than willing to dismiss Jaxon's earlier claims as nonsense until Little came into the room and confirmed at least half of them. That made Stazy question whether or not Jaxon might not be right about the other half too…?

'Little, do you have any idea why my grandfather might be unavailable this evening?'

The butler raised iron-grey brows. 'I had no idea that Sir Geoffrey was unavailable…'

She had known Little for more years than she cared to acknowledge, and had always found him to be quietly efficient and totally devoted to the comfort of both her grandmother and grandfather. Never, during all of those years, had Stazy ever doubted Little's word.

She doubted it now…

There was something about Little's tone—an evasiveness that caused a flutter of sickening unease in the depths of Stazy's stomach. 'Could you please ask Mrs Harris to delay dinner for fifteen minutes or so?' she requested briskly. 'I have several things I need to do before we go through to the dining room.'

This time she was sure that she wasn't imagining it when Little's mouth tightened fractionally in disapproval. 'Very well, Miss Stazy.' He gave her a formal bow before leaving.

But not, Stazy noted frowningly, before he had sent a slightly censorious glance in Jaxon's direction!

'Not a happy man,' Jaxon murmured ruefully as he stood up.

'No,' Stazy agreed softly.

She was obviously more than a little puzzled by this strange turn of events—to the point that Jaxon now felt slightly guilty for having voiced his concerns and causing Stazy's present confusion. Maybe he should have just kept quiet about the arrival of the extra guards and his not being allowed to leave the grounds of Bromley House earlier? And the fact that Geoffrey had been unable to come to the telephone when he'd called. Whatever that obscure statement might mean…

Jaxon certainly regretted the worry he could now see clouding Stazy's troubled green eyes, and the slight pallor that had appeared in the delicacy of her cheeks. 'I'm sure there's no real need for concern, Stazy—'

'You're sure of no such thing, Jaxon, so please stop treating me as if I were a child,' she dismissed. 'Something is seriously wrong here, and I intend to find out exactly what it is!'

After only two days of being in close proximity to Stazy he knew better than to argue with her. Or offer her comfort. He was only too well aware that she was a woman who liked to give the outward appearance of being in control of her emotions, at least.

'And how do you intend to do that…?' he prompted softly.

'By telephoning my grandfather myself, of course.' She moved to where her handbag lay on the floor beside one of the armchairs, taking her mobile from its depths before pressing the button for one of the speed dials. 'I've never been unable to talk to my grandfather—Is that you, Glynis…?' She frowned as the call was obviously answered not by Geoffrey, as she had hoped, but probably the same woman Jaxon had spoken to earlier. 'Yes. Yes, it is. Where—? Oh. I see. Well, do you have any idea when he will be out of the meeting?' She shot Jaxon a frowning glance.

Jaxon gave her privacy for the call by strolling across the room to stand in front of one of the bay windows that looked over the long driveway. The same window, he realised, where Stazy had been standing six weeks ago, and again two days ago, as she had waited for him to arrive…

He had certainly been aware of the existence of Geoffrey and Anastasia Bromley's granddaughter before coming here, but he had in no way been prepared for Stazy's physical resemblance to her grandmother. Since his return to Bromley House he had become aware that that resemblance was more than skin deep; Stazy had the same confidence and self-determination that his earlier research had shown Anastasia to have possessed in spades.

It appeared that the only way in which the two women differed was emotionally…

Not even that self-confidence and strong outer shell were able to hide Stazy's inner emotional vulnerability. A vulnerability that for some reason brought forth every protective instinct in Jaxon's body…

That was pretty laughable when Stazy had made it clear on more than one memorable occasion that he was the last person she wanted to get close to her—emotionally or otherwise!

He turned back into the room now, as he heard her ending the call.

'Everything okay?' he prompted lightly.

She seemed preoccupied as she slipped her mobile back into her bag before straightening. 'My grandfather is in a meeting,' she explained unnecessarily; Jaxon had already ascertained that much from listening to the beginning of Stazy's telephone conversation. 'Glynis will get him to call me back as soon as he comes out.'

'And Glynis is…?'

The frown deepened between Stazy's delicate brows. 'She was his personal secretary until his retirement twenty-five years ago…'

Considering the speed with which those guards had appeared outside Bromley House following the late-night telephone call that had taken Geoffrey up to London two days ago, Jaxon would be very surprised if Geoffrey had ever fully retired.

He gave a shrug. 'Then we may as well go and have dinner while we wait for him to return your call.' He held his arm out to Stazy.

Stazy didn't move, more than a little unsettled by everything that had happened this evening. Those extra guards and her grandfather's unavailability. Little's careful evasion of her questions. Her own feelings of unease at Glynis's claim that her grandfather couldn't speak to her because he was in a meeting. Not once in the fifteen years since Stazy's parents had died had her grandfather ever been too busy to talk to her on the telephone. And why would Glynis be answering Geoffrey's personal mobile at all…?

'It's probably best if you try not to let your imagination run away with you, Stazy.'

She drew herself up determinedly as she realised Jaxon had moved to stand in front of her—so close she could see the beginnings of that dark stubble returning to the squareness of his jaw, and each individual strand of dark hair on his chest revealed by the open neck of his black silk shirt. She could feel the heat of his body, smell the lemon shampoo he had used to wash his hair, and the sandalwood soap he had showered with, all overlaid with a purely male smell that she had come to know was uniquely Jaxon. A smell that always succeeded in making Stazy feel weak at the knees...!

Unless that was just a result of the tensions of these past few minutes?

Who was she trying to fool with these explanation? Herself or Jaxon? If it was herself then she was failing miserably; once again she found it difficult even to breathe properly with Jaxon standing this close to her. And if it was Jaxon she was trying to convince of her uninterest, then the simple act of accepting his arm to go through to the dining room would reveal just how much she was shaking just from his close proximity.

She nodded abruptly as she chose to ignore that proffered arm. 'I'll just go and tell Little we're ready to eat now—if you would like to go through to the dining room?'

Another moment of vulnerability firmly squashed beneath that determined self-control, Jaxon thought ruefully as he gave a brief nod, before lowering his arm and following her from the drawing room. Except Jaxon didn't consider it a vulnerability to acknowledge concern for someone you loved as much as Stazy obviously loved her grandfather...

'Sir Geoffrey is on the telephone,' Little informed them loftily as he came in to the dining room an hour and a half later to remove their dessert plates. 'I took the liberty of transferring the call to his study.'

Stazy stood up abruptly. 'I'll go through immediately—'

'It was Mr Wilder that Sir Geoffrey asked to speak with.' The butler straightened, his gaze fixed steadily on Jaxon rather than on Stazy.

'Mr Wilder?' she repeated dazedly. 'You must be mistaken, Little—'

'Not at all,' the butler assured her mildly. 'I believe you telephoned Sir Geoffrey earlier this evening, sir...?'

Jaxon had to admire the other man's stoicism in the face of Stazy's obvious disbelief of his having correctly relayed the message from Geoffrey Bromley. At the same time he recognised that Stazy's reaction was completely merited; what possible reason could Geoffrey have for asking to speak to Jaxon rather than his own granddaughter? Whatever that reason was, Jaxon doubted it was anything good!

'I did, yes,' he acknowledged lightly as he placed his napkin on the table before standing up. 'If you could just show me to Sir Geoffrey's study...?'

'Certainly, Mr Wilder.'

'Jaxon!'

His shoulders tensed as he turned slowly back to face an obviously less than happy Stazy. Justifiably so, in Jaxon's estimation. Geoffrey had to know that his granddaughter wouldn't just accept his asking to speak with Jaxon rather than her without comment.

'I'm coming with you,' she informed him determinedly.

'I believe Sir Geoffrey wishes to speak with Mr Wilder alone,' Little interjected—bravely, in Jaxon's estimation.

Stazy looked ready to verbally if not physically rip anyone who stood in the way of her talking with her grandfather to shreds. And at the moment Little was definitely attempting to do just that!

Her eyes flashed deeply green as she turned to the butler. 'Sir Geoffrey can wish all he likes, Little,' she assured him firmly. 'But I'm definitely accompanying Mr Wilder to the study!'

Jaxon managed to stand back just in time as Stazy swept past him and out of the room. 'I think that was a pretty predictable reaction, don't you?' he drawled ruefully to the watching butler. 'And, on the positive side, at least I actually got to eat this time before she walked out on me!' The food had been untouched when he had handed the picnic basket back to Little earlier.

'There are times when it is almost possible to believe Lady Anastasia is back with us again...' the other man murmured admiringly as he looked down the hallway at Stazy's retreating and stiffly determined back.

Jaxon nodded. 'Perhaps you had better bring a decanter of brandy and a couple of glasses through to Sir Geoffrey's study in about five minutes...?'

'Certainly, sir.' Little nodded smoothly.

Jaxon strolled down the hallway to where he had seen Stazy enter what had to be Geoffrey Bromley's study, sure that the next few minutes were going to be far from pleasant...

'You heard your grandfather's, Stazy,' Jaxon reminded her gently. 'He said there's absolutely no reason for you to rush up to London just now.'

Stazy was well aware of what her grandfather had said on the telephone, once she had managed to wrest the receiver out of Jaxon's hand and talked to her grandfather herself. Just as she was aware that she had no intention of taking any notice of her grandfather's instruction for her to wait to hear from him again before taking any further action.

Mainly because her grandfather's telephone call had revealed that he had rushed up to London two days ago, and security here had been increased, because he and some members of one of his previous security teams had been receiving threats. That threat had somehow escalated in the past twenty-four hours, and now her grandfather expected—instructed—that she just calmly sit here at Bromley House and await further news!

No way. Absolutely no way was Stazy going to just sit here waiting to see if someone succeeded in attacking her grandfather.

She turned to look at Little as he quietly entered the study with a silver tray containing a decanter of brandy and two glasses. 'I suppose *you* already knew what was going on before we spoke to my grandfather?'

'Stazy,' Jaxon reproved softly from where he sat in the chair facing her grandfather's desk.

'I'm sorry, Little.' Stazy sighed. 'Did you happen to know about these threats to my grandfather?' she asked, less challengingly but just as determinedly, as she watched the butler carefully and precisely place the decanter and glasses on the desktop.

Again Jaxon was sure that he hadn't imagined the butler's reaction—a slight but nevertheless revealing tic in his cheek—before the other man covered his emotion with his usual noncommittal expression as he answered Stazy. 'I believe the increased security measures here are only a precaution, Miss Stazy.'

'I'm not concerned about myself—'

'That will be all, thank you, Little.' Jaxon gave the older man a reassuring smile as he stood up to cross the room and usher the butler out into the hallway before closing the door firmly behind him. 'Taking out your worry concerning your grandfather on one of the people who works for him isn't going to make you feel any better, Stazy.' He spoke mildly as he moved to the front of the desk to pour brandy into the two glasses.

'Is it too much to expect you to understand how worried I feel?' A nerve pulsed in her tightly clenched jaw, and her cheeks were once again pale, her eyes suspiciously over-bright.

With anger or tears, Jaxon wasn't sure…

He straightened slowly to hand her one of the glasses of deep amber liquid. 'No, of course it isn't. I just don't believe insulting Little or me is going to help the situation.'

'Then what is?' She threw the contents of the glass to the back of her throat before moving to refill it.

Jaxon winced. 'Expensive brandies like this one are meant to be breathed in, sipped and then savoured—not thrown down like a pint of unimpressive warm beer!'

'I know that.' She picked up the second glass and took a healthy swallow of the contents of that one too, before slamming it back down on the desk to look up challengingly at Jaxon.

'Stazy, I really wouldn't advise you pushing this situation to a point where I have to use extreme measures in order to calm you down,' Jaxon said softly as he saw the reckless glint in her eyes had deepened.

'Such as what?' she prompted warily. 'Are you going to put me over your knee and spank me for being naughty? Or will just slapping me on the cheek suffice?'

He shrugged. 'I'm not about to slap you anywhere— but the first suggestion has a certain merit at this moment!' Ordinarily Jaxon wouldn't dream of using physical force of any kind on a woman. But this situation was far from ordinary. Stazy was way out of her normally controlled zone. Almost to the point of hysteria. Rightly so, of course, when her grandfather was all the family she had left in the world…

In these unusual circumstances Jaxon didn't at all mind being used as Stazy's verbal punchbag, but he knew her well enough to know that she would be mortified at her treatment of the obviously devoted Little once she had calmed down enough to recognise how she had spoken to him just now—out of love and worry for her grandfather or otherwise.

The uncharacteristic tears glistening in those eyes were his undoing. 'Oh, Stazy…!' he groaned, even as he took her gently into his arms. 'It's going to be okay—you'll see.'

'You don't really know that,' she murmured against his chest as she choked back those tears.

'No, I don't,' Jaxon answered honestly. 'But what I do know is that Geoffrey is a man who knows exactly what he's doing. If he says this problem is going to be handled, then I have no doubt that it will be. And, as you know him much better than I do, you shouldn't either,' he encouraged softly as he ran comforting hands up and down the length of her back.

'You're right. I know you are.' She nodded against him. 'I just—I can't help feeling worried.'

'I know that.' Jaxon's arms tightened about her as the softness of her body rested against the length of his. 'And so does Geoffrey. Which is why he asked me to take care of you.'

She raised her head to look at him, her smile still tearful. 'And this is you taking care of me…?'

'I could possibly do a better job of it if I thought you wouldn't object…?'

Stazy groaned low in her throat as Jaxon slowly lowered his head and slanted his mouth lightly against hers, her body instantly relaxing into his and her fingers becoming entangled in his hair as her lips parted to deepen that kiss.

It felt as if Stazy had been waiting for this to happen since the last time Jaxon had kissed her. Waiting and longing for it. Instantly she became lost to the pleasure of those exploring lips and the caress of Jaxon's hands as they roamed her back before cupping her bottom and pulling her into him.

She was achingly aware of every inch of the lean length of Jaxon's body against hers—his chest hard and unyielding against the fullness of her breasts, the hardness of his erection caught between her stomach and thighs, living evidence of his own rapidly escalating arousal.

Stazy gave another groan as Jaxon's hands tightened about her bottom and he lifted her up and placed her on the edge of the desk. His knees nudged her legs apart, pushing her dress up to her thighs as he stepped between them, and she felt the heat of his erection against the lace of her panties. That groan turned into a low moan of heated pleasure as he pressed into her, applying just the right amount of pressure.

Her neck arched and her fingers clung to the broad width of Jaxon's shoulders when his lips left hers to kiss across her cheek before travelling the length of her throat—kissing, gently biting, as he tasted her creamy skin before his tongue plundered and rasped the sensitive hollows at the base of her neck.

Her back arched as Jaxon's hand moved to cup beneath one of her breasts. The soft material of her dress was no barrier to the pleasure that coursed through her hotly as his thumb moved lightly across the roused and aching nipple, and she was only vaguely aware of it when his other hand slowly lowered the zip of her dress down the length of her spine before his hand touched the naked flesh beneath, revealing that she wasn't wearing a bra.

Jaxon heard the voice in his head telling him to stop this now. Offering Stazy comfort was one thing—what he wanted was something else entirely. He heard that voice and ignored it—had no choice but to ignore it when he could feel how Stazy's pleasure more than matched his own.

He reached up to ease the dress down her arms, baring her to the waist before he moved his hands to cup beneath the swell of her breasts. Such full and heavy breasts, when the rest of her body was so slender. Full and heavy breasts that Jaxon wanted in his mouth as he tasted and pleasured her.

His hands remained firmly on her waist and he moved back slightly to look down at her nakedness. The heat of his gaze on those uptilting breasts tipped by rosy pink and engorged nipples stayed for long, admiring seconds before he lowered his head to take one in his mouth.

Stazy moved her arms so that her hands were flat on the desk behind her, supporting her as the pleasure of having Jaxon's mouth and tongue on her coursed hotly from her breasts to between her thighs. She felt herself tingle there as he took her nipple fully into the heat of his mouth and began to suckle, gently at first, and then more greedily, as his hand cupped her other breast and began to caress her in that same sensuous rhythm.

She was on fire, the ache between her thighs almost unbearable now, building higher and higher, until she knew Jaxon held her poised on the edge of release. 'Please, Jaxon…!' she groaned weakly.

He ignored that plea and instead turned the attentions of his lips, tongue and teeth to her other breast. His lips clamped about the fullness of the nipple as his tongue and teeth licked and rasped against that sensitive bud, driving Stazy wild as she moved her thighs restlessly against his in an effort to ease her aching need for the release that was just a whisper of pleasure away.

She trembled all over with that need, her breath a pained rasp in her throat as she looked down at Jaxon with hot and heavy eyes. Just the sight of his lips clamped about her, drawing her nipple deeper and deeper into his mouth with each greedy suck, caused another rush of heat between her restless and throbbing thighs.

'Jaxon…!' Instead of deepening that pleasure, as she so wanted him to do, it seemed as if Jaxon began to ease away from her, gently kissing her breasts now, his hands once again a soft caress against her back. 'Stop playing with me, please, Jaxon!' she pleaded throatily.

'This isn't a sensible idea, Stazy,' he groaned achingly, even as his arms dropped from about her waist before he straightened away from her.

Stazy looked at him searchingly for several long seconds, easily seeing the regret in his eyes before a shutter came down over those twin mirrors into his emotions. 'Jaxon…?' she breathed softly.

He gave a shake of his head, his expression grim. 'We both know that you're going to end up hating me if I take this any further…'

'You're wrong, Jaxon.' She gave a disbelieving shake of her head, continuing to stare up at him dazedly as she pulled her dress back up her arms to hold it in front of the bareness of her breasts with one hand while she pulled the material down over her naked thighs with the other.

'I am?' he prompted huskily.

'Oh, yes,' Stazy breathed softly. 'Because I couldn't possibly hate you any more than I do at this moment!' Her eyes glittered with humiliated anger now, rather than tears.

Jaxon knew he fully deserved that anger—that he had allowed things to go much further between them just now than was wise when Stazy was already feeling so emotionally vulnerable. But he also knew that Stazy was wrong—she would definitely have hated him more if they had taken their lovemaking to its inevitable conclusion. And on the plus side—for Geoffrey and Little, that was!—Stazy was now far more angry with him than she had been earlier with either of them!

That, in retrospect, was probably the best outcome. He was scheduled to leave here at the end of the week, whereas Geoffrey and Little would both be around for much longer than that.

Jaxon kept his expression noncommittal as he stepped fully away from Stazy, his shaft throbbing in protest as he did so. No doubt another cold shower— a very *long* cold shower!—would be in order when he got back to his suite of rooms. 'There's the possibility you might even thank me for my restraint in the morning...' he murmured ruefully.

'I shouldn't hold your breath on that happening, if I were you!'

'Stazy—'

'I think you should leave now, Jaxon.' It was definitely anger that now sparkled in her eyes.

'Fine,' he accepted wearily. 'But you know where I am if you can't sleep and feel like—'

'Like what?' she cut in sharply. 'I thought we had both just agreed that this was a very bad idea?'

'I was going to say if you feel like company,' Jaxon completed firmly. 'And I don't remembering saying it was a bad idea—just not a very sensible one, given the circumstances.'

'Well, "given the circumstances", I would now like you to leave.' Her chin rose proudly as she held his gaze.

Jaxon gave her one last regretful glance before doing exactly that, knowing that to stay would only make the situation worse.

If that was actually possible…

CHAPTER EIGHT

'THAT really wasn't very clever, now, was it?' Jaxon looked at Stazy impatiently as he entered the drawing room almost two hours later, to see her pacing in front of the bay windows, now dressed in a thick green sweater and fitted black denims, with her red-gold hair neatly plaited down the length of her spine.

She shot him only a cursory glance as she continued to pace restlessly. 'Shouldn't you be fast asleep?'

He closed the door softly behind him. 'Little came and knocked on my bedroom door. He seemed to think I might like to know that you had tried to take my Harley in an attempt to go and see your grandfather tonight.'

'The traitor…'

Jaxon gave a rueful shake of his shaggy head, having quickly pulled on faded denims and a black tee shirt before coming downstairs. 'Exactly when did you take the keys to the Harley off my dressing table…?'

'When I heard the shower running in your bathroom.' She had the grace to look a little guilty. 'I am sorry I took them without your permission, but at the time I didn't feel I had any other choice.'

'Is that your idea of an apology?'

'No.' She sighed. 'It was very wrong of me, and I do

apologise, Jaxon. My grandfather would be horrified if he knew!'

'I'm horrified—but probably not for the same reason!' Jaxon gave her an exasperated glance as he too easily imagined what might have happened if she had managed to ride the Harley. 'How could you even have *thought* taking my motorbike was going to work, Stazy, when there are enough guards patrolling the grounds for them to hear a mouse squeak let alone the roar of an engine starting up?'

'I didn't even get the bike out of the garage,' Stazy acknowledged self-disgustedly.

There had been no excuse for what she had allowed to happen in her grandfather's study earlier that evening, and just thinking about those intimacies once Stazy reached the privacy of her bedroom had been enough to make her want to get as far away from Bromley House—and Jaxon—as possible!

Admittedly it had taken a little time on her part, but once it had occurred to her that she could 'borrow' the keys to Jaxon's Harley and then take the less used and hopefully less guarded back road out of the estate to leave, she hadn't been able to rid herself of the idea.

Unfortunately, as Jaxon had already pointed out, just starting up the engine had brought three of her grandfather's guards running to where the motorbike was parked at the back of the house. Quickly followed by the humiliation of having the keys to the motorbike taken from her before being escorted back inside.

With the added embarrassment that Jaxon now knew exactly what she had planned on doing too. 'Obviously I didn't really think beyond the idea of going to London to see my grandfather,' she accepted guiltily.

'Obviously!' Jaxon gave a disgusted shake of his head. 'You could have been killed, damn it!'

In retrospect Stazy accepted that her method of leaving Bromley House really hadn't been a good plan at all. Not only had starting the engine sounded like the roar of an angry lion in the stillness of the night, but there had still been no guarantee that she would have found it any easier to leave by the back road. She would never know now...

No, in retrospect, taking the Harley hadn't been a good plan at all. And, if Stazy was being honest, she now admitted it had also been an extremely childish one...

Why, oh, why did just being around Jaxon make her behave in this ridiculous way...?

She gave an impatient shake of her head. 'I just feel so—so useless, having to sit here and wait for news from my grandfather.'

Jaxon's expression softened. 'I'm sure Geoffrey is well aware of exactly how you feel, Stazy—'

'Are *you*?' she said warily.

'Yes.' He sighed. 'Look, it's almost one o'clock in the morning, and no doubt the kitchen staff all went to bed hours ago. So why don't the two of us go down to the kitchen and make a pot of tea or something?'

She smiled ruefully. 'Tea being the English panacea for whatever ails you?'

He shrugged. 'It would seem to work in most situations, yes.'

It certainly couldn't do any harm, and Stazy knew she was still too restless to be able to sleep even if she went up to bed now. 'Why not?' she said softly as she crossed the room to precede him out into the hallway.

The house was quiet as Jaxon and Stazy crossed the

cavernous entrance hall on their way to the more shad-
owy hallway that led down to the kitchen, with only the
sound of the grandfather clock ticking to disturb that
eerie silence.

A stark reminder, if Jaxon had needed one, that it
was very late at night and he and Stazy were completely
alone...

And if Stazy believed there had been no repercus-
sions for him after having to walk away from her earlier this evening then she was completely mistaken!

A fifteen-minute cold shower had done absolutely
nothing to dampen Jaxon's arousal. Nor had sitting at
the desk in his bathrobe to read through the notes he
had already accumulated for the screenplay. Or telephoning his agent in LA and chatting to him about it
for ten minutes.

None of those things had done a damned thing to
stop Jaxon's mind from wandering, time and time again,
to thoughts of making love with Stazy in Geoffrey's
study.

As he was thinking about it still...

Self-denial wasn't something Jaxon enjoyed. And
walking away from Stazy—not once, but twice in
the past two days!—was playing havoc with his self-
control!

The cosy intimacy of the warm kitchen and working together to make tea—Jaxon finding the cups while
Stazy filled the kettle with water and switched it on—
did nothing to lessen his awareness of her. Not when
his gaze wandered to her constantly as the slender el-
egance of her hands prepared and warmed the teapot
and he all too easily imagined the places those hands
might touch and caress. The smooth roundness of her

bottom in those black fitted denims wasn't helping either!

'Feeling any better?' Jaxon prompted gruffly, once he was seated on the other side of the kitchen table from Stazy, two steaming cups of tea in front of them.

'Less hysterical, you mean?' She grimaced.

He shook his head. 'You weren't hysterical, Stazy, just understandably concerned about your grandfather.'

'Yes,' she acknowledged with a sigh. 'Still, I didn't have to be quite so bitchy about it.'

'You? Bitchy?' Jaxon gave an exaggerated gasp of disbelief. 'Never!' He placed a dramatic hand on his heart.

She smiled ruefully. 'You aren't going to win any awards with *that* performance!'

'No,' he acknowledged with a wry chuckle.

Stazy sobered. 'Do you think my grandfather is telling us the truth about this threat?' She looked across at him worriedly. 'It occurred to me earlier that he could be using it as a smokescreen,' she continued as Jaxon raised one dark brow. 'That maybe this screenplay and the making of the film might have brought on another heart attack…?'

'Why am I not surprised!' Jaxon grimaced ruefully. 'Do you seriously believe your grandfather would lie to you in that way?'

'If he thought I would worry less, yes,' she confirmed unhesitantly.

Unfortunately, so did Jaxon…

Although he honestly hoped in this instance that wouldn't turn out to be the case. 'Then it's one of those questions where I can't win, however I choose to answer it. If I say no, I can't see that happening, then you aren't going to believe me. And if I say it's a possibility, you'll ask me to consider dropping the whole idea.'

Stazy was rational enough now to be able to see the logic in Jaxon's reply. 'Maybe we should just change the subject…?'

'That might be a good idea,' he drawled ruefully.

She nodded. 'As you probably aren't going to be able to speak to my grandfather about it for several days yet, perhaps you would like to tell *me* what it is you found earlier and wanted to talk to him about…?'

Jaxon gave a wince. 'Another lose/lose question as far as I'm concerned, I'm afraid. And it seems a pity to spoil things when we have reached something of a truce in the last few minutes…'

'It's probably an armed truce, Jaxon,' Stazy said dryly. 'And liable to erupt into shots being exchanged again at any moment!'

'Okay.' He grimaced. 'Curiously, what I've found is something the reporter who wrote the biography seems to have missed altogether…'

'Hmm…'

Jaxon raised one dark brow at that sceptical murmur. 'You don't think he missed it?'

'What I think,' Stazy said slowly, 'is that, whatever you found, my grandfather will have ensured the reporter didn't find it.'

'You believe Geoffrey has that much power…?'

'Oh, yes.' She smiled affectionately.

Jaxon shook his head. 'You don't even know what this is about yet.'

She shrugged. 'I don't need to. If my grandfather left some incriminating papers in the library for you to look at then he meant for you to find them.'

That made Jaxon feel a little better, at least. 'There were two things, actually, but they're related.'

Stazy looked down at her fingertip, running it distractedly around the rim of her cup as she waited for him to continue.

He sighed. 'I found your grandparents' marriage certificate for February 1946.'

'Yes?'

'And your father's birth certificate for October 1944.'

'Yes?'

'Leaving a discrepancy of sixteen months.'

'Two years or more if you take into account the nine months of pregnancy,' she corrected ruefully.

'Yes…'

The tension eased out of Stazy's shoulders as she smiled across at him. 'I'm sure that there are always a lot of children born with questionable birth certificates during war years.'

'No doubt.' Jaxon was literally squirming with discomfort now. 'But—'

'But my father's place of birth is listed as Berlin, Germany,' she finished lightly.

'Yes.' Jaxon breathed his relief.

'With no name listed under the "Father" column.'

'No…'

'Meaning there's no way of knowing for certain that Geoffrey was actually his father.'

'I didn't say that—'

'You didn't have to.' Stazy chuckled. 'It would have looked a little odd, don't you think, to have the name of an Englishman listed as the father of a baby boy born in Berlin in 1944?'

'Well, yes…But—'

'More tea, Jaxon?' She stood up to put more hot

water into the teapot before coming back to stand with the pot poised over his cup.

'Thanks,' he accepted distractedly. He had been dreading having to talk to any of the Bromley family about his discovery earlier today, and especially the unpredictable Stazy. Now, instead of being her usual defensive self, she actually seemed to find the whole thing amusing. To the point that he could see laughter gleaming in those expressive green eyes as she refilled his cup before sitting down again. 'Like to share what's so amusing…?'

'You are.' She gave a rueful shake of her head as she resumed her seat. 'You're aged in your mid-thirties, Jaxon, a Hollywood A-list actor and director, and yet you seem scandalised that there might have been babies born out of wedlock seventy years ago!' She grinned across at him.

'I'm not in the least scandalised—'

'Um…protesting too much, much?' she teased, in the manner of one of her students.

Jaxon eyed her frustatedly. 'These are your grand-parents we're talking about. And your father.'

'Geoffrey and Anastasia never tried to hide from me that my father was actually present and sixteen months old at the time of their wedding,' she assured him gently. 'We have the photographs to prove it. Which I can show you tomorrow—later today,' she corrected, after a glance at the kitchen clock revealed it was now almost two o'clock in the morning. 'If you would like to see them?'

'I would, yes.'

She nodded. 'I'll look them out in the morning.'

'So what happened?' Jaxon said slowly. 'Why didn't

the two of them marry when Anastasia knew she was expecting Geoffrey's child?'

'They didn't marry earlier because Anastasia didn't know she was pregnant when she was dropped behind enemy lines in late February 1944. By the time she realised her condition she had already established her cover as a young Austrian woman, recently widowed and bitterly resentful of the English as a result, and it was too late for her to do anything but remain in Berlin and continue with the mission she had been sent there to complete. She always maintained her pregnancy actually helped to confirm that identity.'

'My God...' Jaxon fell back against his chair.

'Yes.' Stazy smiled affectionately. 'Of course my grandfather, once informed of Anastasia's condition, ensured that she was ordered out of Berlin immediately.'

'And she refused to leave until she had finished what she went there to do?' Jaxon guessed.

Stazy met his gaze unblinkingly. 'Yes, she did.'

'She went through her pregnancy, gave birth to her son, cared for him, all the while behind enemy lines under a false identity that could have been blown apart at any moment?'

Her chin tilted. 'Yes.'

He gave an incredulous shake of his head. 'God, that's so—so—'

'Irresponsible? Selfish?' There was a slight edge to Stazy's voice now.

'I was going to say romantic.' Jaxon grinned admiringly. 'And incredibly brave. What a woman she must have been!'

Stazy relaxed slightly as she answered huskily, 'I've always believed so, yes.'

Jaxon nodded. 'And so you should. You're very like her, you know,' he added softly.

'I don't think so, Jaxon.' Stazy gave a choked laugh. 'Even in her nineties Anastasia would have made sure she got on that Harley tonight and somehow managed to ride it out of here, despite all those guards trying to stop her!'

'Maybe,' he acknowledged dryly. 'But you definitely gave it your best shot.'

She shrugged. 'Not good enough, obviously.'

'Choosing the Harley for your first attempt was extremely gutsy.' In fact Stazy's behaviour tonight was so much more than Jaxon would ever have believed possible of that stiffly formal and tightly buttoned down Dr Anastasia Bromley he had been introduced to six weeks ago. 'So you think Geoffrey meant for me to find the marriage and birth certificates…?'

She nodded. 'I'm sure of it.'

'Why?'

Stazy gave a rueful smile. 'For some reason he seems to trust you to do the right thing…' she said slowly, knowing there was no way her grandfather would ever have put the reputation of his darling Anastasia in the hands of a man he didn't trust implicitly.

Something she should probably have appreciated more while resenting Jaxon these past six weeks…

He leant across the table now, to take one of her hands gently in both of his. 'And do *you* trust me to do that too, Stazy?'

She did trust him, Stazy realised as she looked across the table at him. That silver-grey gaze was unmistakably sincere as it met hers unwaveringly.

Yes, she trusted Jaxon—it was herself she didn't trust whenever she was around him!

Even now, worried about her grandfather, frustrated at not being able to leave the estate, Stazy was totally aware of Jaxon as he held her hand in both of his. Of the roughness of his palm, the gentleness of his fingers as they played lightly across the back of her hand, sending a quiver of awareness through her arm and down into the fullness of her breasts and between her thighs. Warming her. Once again arousing her...

'I trust my grandfather's judgement in all things,' she finally said huskily.

'But not mine?' Jaxon said shrewdly.

Stazy pulled her trembling hand out of his grasp before pushing it out of sight beneath the table, very aware of the heat of awareness singing through her veins. 'It's late, Jaxon.' She stood up abruptly. 'And tomorrow looks as if it's going to be something of a long and anxious day. We should at least try to get some sleep tonight.' She picked up their empty cups and carried them over to the sink to rinse them out before placing them on the rack to dry.

All the time she was aware of Jaxon's piercing gaze on her. Heating her blood to boiling point. Her legs trembled slightly, so that she was forced to resort to leaning against the sink unit for support.

'Stazy...?'

She drew in a deep breath, desperately searching for some of the coolness and control that had stood her in such good stead these past ten years. Searching and failing.

'If something I've said or done has upset you, then I apologise...'

Stazy had been so deeply entrenched in fighting the heat of her emotions that she hadn't even been aware that Jaxon had moved to stand behind her. The warmth of his breath was now a gentle caress as it brushed against the tendrils of hair at her nape that had escaped the neatness of her plait. If he should so much as touch her—!

She slipped away from that temptation before turning to face him. 'You haven't done anything to upset me, Jaxon,' she assured him crisply. 'I think it's as you implied earlier—I'm just emotionally overwrought.'

Jaxon could see the evidence of exhaustion in the dark shadows beneath her eyes. Her cheeks were pale, those full and vulnerable lips trembling slightly as she obviously fought against giving in to that exhaustion. 'Time for bed,' he agreed firmly, before taking a tight grip of her hand and leading her gently across the room to the doorway, switching off the kitchen light on his way out.

He retained that firm grip on the delicacy of her hand as the two of them walked down the shadowed hallway and up the wide staircase together, allowing him to feel the way her fingers tightened about his and her steps seemed to slow as they approached the top of the stairs.

Jaxon turned to look at Stazy in the semi-darkness. Her eyes were deeply green and too huge in the paleness of her face. 'Stazy, would you rather have company tonight…?' Even though he spoke softly his voice still sounded over-loud in the stillness of the dark night surrounding them.

Stazy came to an abrupt halt at the top of the stairs, frowning as she turned to look at him searchingly, the contours of his face sharply hewn in the moonlight, the expression in his eyes totally unreadable with those grey eyes hooded by long dark lashes and lowered lids. 'Exactly what are you suggesting, Jaxon…?' she finally murmured warily.

'I'm asking if you would like me to come to your bedroom and spend the rest of the night with you,' he bit out succinctly.

Exactly what Stazy had thought he was offering! 'Why?'

Jaxon chuckled softly. 'How about because I know how the hours between two o'clock in the morning and five o'clock can sometimes be tough to get through if you have something on your mind.'

Stazy raised auburn brows. 'Are you talking from personal experience?'

He gave a hard grin. 'Difficult as you obviously find that to believe, yes, I am. Never anything as serious as your present concerns over your grandfather, but I've definitely had my fair share of worries over the years.'

'Things like looking in the mirror for the first grey hair and wrinkle?' she came back teasingly.

'Hair dye and botox injections,' Jaxon came back dismissively.

Her eyes widened. 'Have you ever—?'

'No, I can honestly say I've never resorted to using either one of those things!' he assured her irritably, seeing her obvious humour at his expense.

'Yet.'

'Ever,' Jaxon assured firmly. 'I'm going to live by the adage and grow old gracefully.'

Stazy knew he was teasing her—was very aware that these last few minutes they'd both been talking only for the sake of it. Delaying as they waited to see what her answer was going to be to Jaxon's offer to spend the night with her...

'Well?' Jaxon prompted huskily.

He claimed he was making the offer so that she didn't have to spend the hours before dawn alone; and God knew Stazy didn't want to *be* alone, knowing that once she was in her bedroom her imagination was going to run riot again in regard to her grandfather's safety. Did that mean she was actually thinking of *accepting* Jaxon's offer to spend the night with her...?

CHAPTER NINE

'I PREFER to sleep on the right side of the bed.'

'So do I.'

'It's my bedroom.'

'And, as your guest, don't you think I should be allowed first choice as to which side of the bed I would like to sleep on?'

'Not if my guest is a gentleman.'

As conversations before leaping into bed with a man went, this one was pretty pathetic, Stazy acknowledged self-derisively. No doubt due in part to the fact that now they were actually at the point of getting into bed she was awash with flustered embarrassment.

To a degree that she questioned which part of her brain had actually been functioning when she had accepted Jaxon's offer to spend the night in her bedroom with her. Certainly not the logical and ordered Dr Stazy Bromley part! And even the less logical, easily-aroused-by-Jaxon-Wilder, Stazy Bromley now questioned the sanity of that decision too!

It had been an impulsive decision at best, made out of a desire not to lie alone in the darkness for hours with her own worried thoughts.

Having just returned from the adjoining bathroom in a white vest top and the grey sweats she slept in, she

saw the soft glow of the bedside lamp revealed that
Jaxon wore only a pair of very brief black underpants
that clearly outlined the enticing bulge beneath. His bare
shoulders were wide and tanned, chest muscled and
abdomen taut, his legs long and muscular and equally
tanned, allowing Stazy to fully appreciate just how ri-
diculously naive that decision had been.

Especially when her clenched fingers actually itched
with the need she felt to touch the fine dark hair that
covered his chest before it arrowed down in an enticing vee to beneath those fitted black underpants...

'Perhaps you should go to your bedroom first and
get some pyjamas...' she said doubtfully—as if Jaxon
wearing pyjamas was *really* going to make her any less
aware of his warmth in the bed beside her!

'That would probably be a good idea if I actually
wore pyjamas.' Jaxon eyed her mockingly across the
width of the double bed.

Right. Okay. Definitely time to regroup, Stazy. 'In
that case you can have the right side of the bed—'

'I was just kidding about that, Stazy,' Jaxon drawled
softly when she would have walked around to the side
of the bed where he stood. 'The left side of the bed is
fine.'

To say he had been surprised by her acceptance of
his offer was putting it mildly. That only went to prove
that Stazy was even more complex than he had thought
she was. To the point that Jaxon had no idea what she
was going to do or say next. That was very refreshing
from a male point of view, but damned inconvenient
when a man was only supposed to be acting as a concerned friend...

For some reason he had expected her to be wearing one of those unbecoming nightgowns that covered

a woman from neck to toe when she came back from the bathroom. Instead she wore a thin white fitted top with narrow shoulder straps, clearly outlining her up-thrusting and obviously naked breasts, and in the process allowing Jaxon to see every curve and nuance of her engorged nipples, along with a pair of loose grey soft cotton trousers that rested low down on her hips and gave him the occasional glimpse of the flat curve of her stomach. The cherry on top of the cake—as if he needed one!—was that she had released the long length of her red-gold hair from its plait and it now lay in a soft and silky curtain across her shoulders and down her back.

All of them were things that were pure purgatory for any man who was expected to behave only as a friend...

He should be grateful Stazy had a double bed in her room, he supposed; just think how cosy the two of them would have been in a single bed! Even so, Jaxon was well aware of how much space he was going to take up, so it was perhaps as well that Stazy was so slender.

He quirked one dark brow as he looked across the bed at her. 'Are we going to get in and get warm, or just stand here looking at each other all night?'

Stazy drew in a slightly shaky breath. 'Perhaps your spending the night here wasn't such a good idea, after all—Oh!' She broke off as Jaxon lifted his side of the duvet before sliding in beneath it to look up at her expectantly.

'It's much warmer in here than it is out there...' he encouraged, and turned the duvet back invitingly.

Stazy wasn't sure any extra warmth was necessary. She already felt inwardly on fire, her cheeks flushed, the palms of her hands slightly damp.

Oh, for goodness' sake—

'Better,' Jaxon murmured as Stazy finally slid into the bed beside him.

She turned to look at him as she straightened the duvet over her. 'Is that a statement or a question?'

'Both,' he assured her softly, before reaching out to turn off the bedside lamp and plunge the room into darkness. His arms moved about her waist as he pulled her in to his side and gently pressed her head down onto the warmth of his shoulder.

Stazy didn't feel in the least relaxed. How could she possibly relax when she was snuggled against Jaxon's warm and almost naked body, her fingers finally able to touch the silkily soft hair on his chest as her hand lay against that hardness encased in velvet, her elbow brushing lightly against that telling bulge in his underpants?

This had *so* not been a good idea. She was never going to be able to relax, let alone—

'Just close your eyes and go to sleep, Stazy,' Jaxon instructed huskily in the darkness.

Her throat moved as she swallowed before answering him softly. 'I'm not sure that I can.'

'Close your eyes? Or go to sleep?'

'Either!'

'I could always sing you a lullaby, I suppose...'

'I didn't know you could sing...'

'I can't.' His chest vibrated against her cheek as he chuckled, then Jaxon's hand moved up to cradle the back of her head as it rested against his shoulder. He settled more comfortably into the pillows. 'This is nice.'

Nice? It was sheer heaven as far as Stazy was concerned! Decadent and illicit pleasure. A time out of time, when it felt as if only the two of them existed.

Those 'witching hours' between dusk and dawn when anything—everything!—seemed possible.

'Stop fidgeting, woman,' Jaxon instructed gruffly when she shifted restlessly beside him.

Or not, Stazy acknowledged ruefully. 'I was just getting comfortable.'

When a man wanted a woman as much as Jaxon wanted Stazy, her 'getting comfortable' could just be the last straw in the breaking of his self-control. Especially when that 'getting comfortable' involved her hair spilling silkily across his chest, the softness of her breasts pressing into his side, and the draping of one of her legs over the top of his.

Her hand rested lightly on his stomach as she snuggled closer to his warmth… 'What's that noise…?' she murmured sleepily minutes later.

'Probably my teeth grinding together.'

'Why—?'

'Will you please just go to sleep!' Jaxon's jaw was tightly clenched as he determinedly held his desire for her in check.

'I thought people were usually grouchy when they woke up in the morning, not before they've even gone to sleep…'

Jaxon had a feeling he was going to be grouchy in the morning too—probably more so than he was now, if he had been lying beside Stazy all night with a throbbing erection! Worst of all, he had brought all this on himself, damn it. 'I'll try not to disappoint,' he murmured self-derisively.

Stazy chuckled sleepily, and the evenness of her breathing a few minutes later told him that she had managed to fall asleep after all.

Leaving Jaxon awake and staring up at the ceiling

in the darkness, in the full knowledge that he wasn't going to be able to find the same release from his own self-imposed purgatory...

Arousal.
    Instant.
    Breathtaking.
    Joyous!
    'Are you awake...?' Jaxon prompted softly.
    'Mmm...' Stazy kept her eyes closed as she relished the sensation of Jaxon's large and capable hands moving lightly, slowly over her and down her body, as if he intended to commit every curve and contour to memory.
    Her back. The soft curve of her bottom. Skimming across her hips. The gentle slope of her waist. Her ribcage and up over her breasts. Until he cupped the side of her face, his fingertips moving lightly across the plumpness of her parted lips before running lightly down the length of her throat to dip into the hollows at its base. Those same fingers ran a light caress over her clavicle, before pushing the thin strap from her shoulder and down her arm, tugging gently on the material of her top until one plump, aroused breast popped free of its confinement.
    Stazy gave a breathless gasp as she arched into that large and cupping hand, its thumb and index finger lightly rolling the engorged bud at its tip before tugging gently. Pleasure coursed through her hotly as Jaxon alternated those rhythmic caresses for several agonisingly pleasurable minutes before the hot and moist sweep of his tongue laved that throbbing nipple.
    'Jaxon...!' Her eyes were wide open now, and she looked down at him in the early-morning sunlight, the darkness of his hair a tousled caress against her flesh,

those grey eyes smoky with arousal as he glanced up at her. 'Please don't stop this time...!' she encouraged achingly.

One of her hands moved up to cradle the back of his head and her fingers became entangled in the overlong darkness of his hair as she held him to her.

Pleasure lit his eyes before he turned his attention back to her breast, alternately licking, biting and gently suckling, before moving across to bestow that same pleasure upon its twin.

His skin was so much darker than hers as he nudged her legs apart and moved to settle between her parted thighs, all hard muscle and sinew where her hands moved caressingly down the length of his spine. Stazy was totally aware of the long length of his arousal pressing into her as her hands dipped beneath his black underpants to cup the muscled contours of his bottom.

Jaxon's hands tightly gripped Stazy's hips as he raised his head to draw in a hissing breath. Those slender hands squeezed and caressed him, turning his body slightly, and he encouraged those hands to move to the front of his body, ceasing to breathe at all as long and slender fingers curved around his shaft and the soft pad of her thumb ran lightly over the moisture escaping its tip.

He had fallen asleep fitfully, only to wake mere hours later. Stazy had continued to sleep. His body had been hard and aching, and finally he hadn't been able to resist waking her. He had needed to touch her—just a light caress or two, he had promised himself. And so he had caressed her hips. Her stomach. Her throat.

That was when he had lost it, Jaxon acknowledged achingly. The arching of Stazy's body into that caress had been more than his control could withstand, and the pulse of his shaft grew harder as he'd suckled her greedily into his mouth.

And now, at the first touch of her fingers on him, Jaxon felt as if he was about to explode—

'Lie back, Jaxon, and let me take these off for you,' Stazy encouraged huskily, and she pushed him back against the pillows before moving up onto her knees beside him, pulling off the tangle of her top to ease her movements before sitting forward to slowly pull his black underpants down over his hips and thighs. His eyes were riveted on her naked breasts as they bobbed forward enticingly, and he groaned low in his throat as his throbbing shaft was at last allowed to jut free as she discarded his underpants completely before looking down at him with greedy eyes.

Jaxon groaned again as he saw her tongue appear between those pouting lips before moving over them moistly. If Stazy so much as touched him with those wet and pouting lips then he was going to—

'Oh, dear God…!' Jaxon's hips lifted up off the bed as Stazy lowered her head, one of her hands once again firmly grasping his shaft and the other cupping him beneath, and her lips parted widely as she took him completely into the heat of her mouth, licking, sucking, savouring…

He could smell Stazy's arousal now—a hot and musky scent that drove his own pleasure higher than ever as her tongue laved him, fingers lightly pumping, before she took him fully into her mouth and sucked him deep into the back of her throat.

It was too much—Stazy was too much!

'You have to stop. Now!' Jaxon gripped her shoulders as he pulled her up and away from him, allowing the full heaviness of his shaft to fall damply against

the hardness of his stomach. 'It's my turn,' he assured
her huskily as he saw the questioning disappointment
in her eyes, and he laid her gently back against the pillows and moved to roll the last piece of clothing from
her body, sitting back on his haunches to look down at
the pearly perfection of her naked body: pale ivory skin,
the fullness of her breasts tipped with those ruby-red
nipples, a red-gold thatch of curls between her thighs.

His nudge was gentle as he parted her legs to kneel
between her thighs and reveal her hidden beauty to him.
He enjoyed Stazy's groan of pleasure as he ran the tips
of his fingers over and around her sensitive bud before
lowering his head to move his tongue against her, again
and again, until she arched into him as he gently suckled her into his mouth.

Stazy gave a low and torturous moan as Jaxon's finger caressed and probed her moist and swollen opening before sliding gently inside her, quickly joined by a
second. Those muscled walls clasped around him and
he began to thrust into her with the same rhythm as his
suckling mouth. Stazy arched into those thrusts, needing, wanting—

Pleasure coursed hotly, fiercely through her as she
began to orgasm. There was a loud roaring sound in
her ears and a kaleidoscope of coloured lights burst behind her eyelids as ecstatic release ripped through her
for long, relentless minutes. Jaxon gave no quarter as
he coaxed the last shuddering spasm of pleasure from
her boneless and replete body before finally releasing
her, to lay his head against her thigh.

That was when Stazy became aware she still had that
loud roaring noise in her ears. Her eyes opened wide as
she looked down at Jaxon dazedly. 'What...?'

He raised his head lazily, eyes dark, lips moist and

full. 'I'd really like to take credit for being the cause of that phenomena, but I'm afraid I can't,' he murmured ruefully.

Stazy looked about the bedroom dazedly, completely disorientated—both by the satiated weakness she felt following the fierceness of her first ever orgasm, and by that loud, inexplicable roaring in her ears.

Her gaze returned to Jaxon when she could find no possible reason for that noise in the neatness of her bedroom. 'What is it?' she breathed huskily.

Jaxon had a feeling he knew exactly what it was. *Who* it was. Just as he knew it was a presence guaranteed to wipe away that look of satiation from the relaxed beauty of Stazy's face!

He gave Stazy's naked and satisfied body one last regretful glance before levering up onto his elbows and knees and crawling off the end of the bed to stroll over to the window. He twitched aside one of the curtains to look down on to the manicured lawn below.

'Yep, I was afraid of that.' He grimaced, letting the curtain fall back into place as he turned back to where Stazy now sat on the side of the bed, looking across at him with wide, still slightly dazed eyes.

'Afraid of what?' She gave a puzzled shake of her head.

Jaxon drew in a heavy breath before answering her. 'It's your grandfather. He's just arrived by helicopter,' he added, as Stazy still looked completely dazed.

Her eyes widened in alarm. 'He— I— You— We—' She threw back the bedclothes to stand up abruptly, completely unconcerned by her nakedness—and Jaxon's, regrettably!—as she hurried across the room to pull one of the curtains aside for herself. 'Oh, dear Lord…!' she groaned, obviously in a complete panic as she quickly dropped the curtain back over the window and turned to grasp Jaxon's arm. 'We have to get dressed! No—first you need to go back to your own bedroom!' She released his arm to commence frantically gathering his discarded clothes up off the carpet, before screwing them up into a bundle and shoving them at his chest. 'You need to take these with you—'

'Will you just calm down, Stazy?' Jaxon took the clothes from her and placed them on the bedside chair, before reaching out to grasp both her arms and shake her gently. 'You're twenty-nine years old, for goodness' sake—'

'And that's my grandfather out there!' Her eyes had taken on a hunted look.

'We haven't done anything wrong,' he said soothingly.

'If this were my apartment, or a hotel, then I would be inclined to agree with you—but this is *Gramps'* home!' She was breathing hard in her agitation, her face white against the deep green of her eyes as she hurried through to the adjoining bathroom to return with her robe seconds later.

'Stazy, I very much doubt that the first thing Geoffrey is going to do when he enters the house is come up to your bedroom to see if by some chance we might have spent the night together in his absence—'

'Please don't argue any more—just go, Jaxon!' She looked up at him pleadingly after tying the belt to her robe.

'I have every intention of going back to my own bedroom, Stazy,' he assured gruffly. 'But I think I should dress first, don't you? Rather than risk bumping into your grandfather or one of the household staff in the hallway when I'm completely naked...?'

He had a point, Stazy accepted with a pained wince. She hadn't expected— It hadn't even occurred to her— She hadn't been thinking clearly at all last night when she had agreed to Jaxon's coming to her bedroom and spending the night with her!

And her explanation—her excuse for what had happened with Jaxon this morning...?

She didn't have one. At least not one that she wanted to think about right now. She couldn't think at all now— not with her grandfather about to enter Bromley House!

'Nor,' Jaxon continued grimly, 'do I find it in the least acceptable to sneak out of your bedroom like a naughty schoolboy caught in the act!'

Stazy winced at the obvious displeasure in his tone. 'I wasn't implying that—'

'No?' He turned away to sort impatiently through the pile of clothes on the bedroom chair, giving Stazy a breathtaking view of the bare length of his back and the tautness of his buttocks as he pulled on those fitted black underpants. 'It seems to me that's exactly what you're implying.' His expression was bleak as he un- hurriedly pulled on the rest of his clothes before sitting down on the side of the bed to lace his shoes.

'Look, we can talk about this later, Jaxon—?'

'What is there to talk about?' He stood up, tower- ing over Stazy as she stood barefoot in front of him. 'In my profession I've learnt that actions invariably speak louder than words, Stazy,' he bit out harshly. 'And your actions, your haste to get rid of me, tell me that you re- gret what just happened—'

'And *you're* behaving like that ridiculous school- boy—' She broke off as she saw the thunderous dark- ness of Jaxon's frown. His eyes were a pale and glittering grey as he looked down the length of his nose at her, a nerve pulsed in his tightly clenched jaw.

'Just forget it, Stazy,' he bit out bleakly.

Forget it? Forget that amazing, wonderful lovemaking? Forget that she had wanted Jaxon enough, trusted him enough, to share her first ever orgasm with him…?

That alone was enough to tell Stazy how inconsequential her two sexual experiences had been. Just how much of herself she had held back from those other men…

Just now, with Jaxon, she had been completely open. The barriers that she had kept erected about her emotions for so many years had come crashing down around her ears as she gave herself up completely to the pleasure of Jaxon's lips and hands on her body.

Meaning what, exactly?

She couldn't actually have come to *care* for Jaxon over these past few days alone with him, could she?

And by care, did she mean—?

No!

She wasn't going there!

Not now.

Not ever!

Jaxon was an accomplished and experienced lover— a man used to making a conquest of any woman he went to bed with. Those were the reasons—the only reasons!—for her own loss of control just now.

Her chin rose proudly. 'Fine, then I guess we won't talk later,' she said dismissively.

Jaxon looked down at Stazy from between narrowed lids, wishing he knew what thoughts had been going through her head during those few minutes of silence, but as usual her closed expression revealed none of her inner emotions to him.

He probably shouldn't have been so annoyed with her just now. No—he *definitely* shouldn't have been annoyed with her just now! His only excuse was that it had been irritating, galling, to be made to feel like a guilty indiscretion as far as Stazy was concerned—especially when he could still feel the silkiness of her skin against his hands and taste her on his lips and tongue. When he was aware that he was starting to care for her in a way he had never imagined when they had met six weeks ago...

'I really think you should go now, Jaxon.' Stazy backed away from the hand he had raised with the intention of reaching out and caressing her cheek.

Jaxon's hand dropped back to his side and he looked down at her searchingly for several long seconds before nodding abruptly. 'But we will talk about this again before I leave here,' he promised softly, his gaze intent, before he turned on his heel and crossed to the door, letting himself quietly out of the room.

Stazy felt awash with regret as she watched Jaxon close the bedroom door behind him as he left, having to bite down painfully on her bottom lip to stop herself from calling out to prevent him from going.

What would be the point of stopping him? Their lovemaking, her pleasure, might have been life-altering for her, but as far as Jaxon was concerned she had merely been another sexual interlude in his life...

CHAPTER TEN

'AND that, I'm afraid, is my reason for not telling you both yesterday evening that I was actually in hospital, having stitches put in my arm, when I spoke to you on the telephone.' Geoffrey concluded his explanation ruefully as he turned from where Jaxon stood in front of one of the bay windows in the drawing room to look concernedly at his still and silent granddaughter as she sat in the armchair opposite near the unlit fireplace.

It was an explanation Jaxon thought worthy of one of the dozens of film scripts presented to him every year!

Death threats from an unknown assassin. Gunshots in the night. The apprehension and arrest of a gunman by the security men who had been guarding Geoffrey in London. A gunman, it transpired, who held an old and personal grudge against Geoffrey, but had been unaware of exactly how and where to find him until he had seen and read that appalling biography on Anastasia published the previous year.

'You were shot at…?' Stazy was the one to break the silence, deathly white as she sat unmoving in the armchair.

Her grandfather looked down at the sling on his right arm. 'It's only a flesh wound.'

Stazy stood up abruptly. 'Someone actually shot you

and you chose not to tell me about it?' She still found it unbelievable her grandfather could have done such a thing. Or, in this case, *not* done such a thing!

Absolutely unbelievable!

'Well…yes.' Geoffrey gave a regretful wince. 'I didn't want to alarm you—'

'You didn't want to alarm me…!' Stazy breathed hard as she looked down at her grandfather incredulously. 'I don't believe you, Gramps!' she finally snapped exasperatedly. 'Some unknown man has been stalking you—only you!—for days now, he finally succeeded in managing to shoot you, and you decided not to tell me about it because you didn't want to *alarm* me!'

The same night she had spent in Jaxon's arms…

'I did tell you of a threat—'

'But not to you personally.'

'No, but—'

'Admit it, Gramps, you lied to me!' she accused emotionally, her cheeks burning.

'Stazy—'

'Don't even attempt to offer excuses for his behaviour, Jaxon,' she warned hotly when he would have interceded. 'There are no excuses. I was worried to death about you, Gramps.' She rounded back on her grandfather.

'Telling you I had been shot would only have worried you even more—'

'I'm not sure that was even possible!' She gave an exasperated shake of her head. 'I'm sorry, but if I stay here any longer then I'm going to say something I'll really regret. If you will both excuse me?' She didn't wait for either man to answer before rushing from the room.

'Well, that didn't go too well, did it?' Geoffrey

murmured ruefully as the door slammed behind Stazy with barely controlled violence.

'Not too well, no,' Jaxon confirmed dryly as he turned back from admiring how beautiful Stazy had looked as she left the room. That red-gold hair had seemed to crackle with electricity, her eyes had glittered like emeralds, her creamy cheeks had been flushed. The cream silk blouse and close-fitting denims she was wearing today weren't too hard on the eye either!

'Why doesn't she understand that I was only trying to protect her by not telling her the truth until the whole thing was over and done with?' the older man asked in obvious frustration.

Jaxon grimaced as he stepped further into the room, having deemed it safer to stand a little removed while granddaughter and grandfather confronted each other. 'I may be wrong, but I believe Stazy considers herself to be a little old to still be in need of that sort of protection from you or anyone else.'

'And what do you think I could have done differently in the circumstances?' Geoffrey frowned up at him.

Jaxon gave a rueful smile. 'I'm the last person you should be asking about how best to deal with Stazy.'

'Indeed?' Geoffrey's gaze sharpened speculatively.

'Oh, yes!' he said with feeling.

'Does that mean the two of you are still at loggerheads?' the older man frowned again.

Jaxon wasn't sure how his relationship with Stazy stood at this precise moment. Last night she had allowed him to comfort her. This morning they had almost made love to each other. Before having the most god-awful row when Geoffrey had arrived so unexpectedly!

No, Jaxon had no idea how Stazy felt towards him now.

Any more than he knew what to make of his feelings for her...

It had been both heaven and hell to hold Stazy in his arms all night long, and sheer unadulterated pleasure to be with her this morning.

Knowing how Stazy liked to keep her life compartmentalised and Jaxon didn't, the argument that had followed had perhaps been predictable—but that didn't stop it from being frustrating as hell as far as Jaxon was concerned.

Where the two of them went from here—if they went anywhere—Jaxon had absolutely no idea.

'More or less, yes,' he answered the older man abruptly.

'Do I want to know how much more or how much less...?' Geoffrey prompted softly.

Jaxon gave the question some thought. 'Probably not,' he finally answered carefully.

The other man looked at him searchingly for several long seconds before giving a slow nod of his head. 'Okay. So, do you think Stazy will ever forgive me...?'

Probably a lot more quickly than she was going to forgive Jaxon—if she ever did forgive him! 'I think it might be a good idea if you give her some time to— well, to calm down before attempting to talk to her again,' he advised ruefully.

'And in the meantime...?'

'I have absolutely no idea *what* you do in the meantime.' Jaxon grimaced. 'But now that security here has been lifted I intend to change into my leathers and go out for a ride on the Harley,' he said decisively.

'I'd ask to join you, but I think that might push Stazy into disowning me completely!' Geoffrey chuckled wryly.

'There's no "might" about it!' Jaxon assured him.

The older man nodded slowly. 'Let's hope she decides to forgive me very soon.'

It was a hope Jaxon echoed…

Stazy stood with her forehead pressed against the coolness of her bedroom window, looking outside as the Harley roared off down the gravel driveway with a leather-clad Jaxon seated on the back of it, the black helmet once again covering his almost shoulder-length hair and the smoky visor lowered over his face. Although it wasn't too difficult for her to imagine the grimness of his expression!

Was Jaxon leaving for good? Or had he just gone out for a drive now that there was no longer a reason for them to be confined to Bromley House?

Not that Stazy could altogether blame Jaxon if he *had* decided to leave. A part of her knew she would have to leave too. And soon. She longed for the peace and solitude of her apartment in London, desperately needed to be alone for a while—if only so that she could lick her wounds in private. At the same time she knew she couldn't leave here until things were less strained between herself and her grandfather.

How could he have lied to her in that way? Oh, she could appreciate the reason her grandfather had thought he should skirt around the truth, but that didn't mean Stazy had to be in the least understanding about his having so blatantly lied to her at the end.

Especially when those lies had resulted in her spending the night with Jaxon…

Damn it, spending the night with Jaxon hadn't been the problem—it had been waking up in his arms this morning and the things that had followed that made her cringe with embarrassment every time she so much as thought about it! Which had been often during the half an hour or so she had spent in her bedroom.

Thankfully the maid had been up to Stazy's bedroom during her absence downstairs, so the bed had been neatly remade and the room tidied by the time she returned from talking with her grandfather. Unfortunately, as Stazy had crossed the bedroom to take her suitcase out of the wardrobe and place it on top of the bed, that neatness had done very little to stop her from remembering each and every detail of what had happened here between herself and Jaxon...

The joy of kissing and caressing him. The pleasure of being kissed and caressed *by* him. The unimagined ecstasy of the mind-blowing orgasm he had so easily taken her to...

Even now Stazy could feel the ultra-sensitivity between her legs in the aftermath of her orgasm. Her first ever orgasm...

And her last if it resulted in her not only feeling physically vulnerable but emotionally too!

Although Jaxon's abrupt departure—without that promised talk between the two of them—would seem to imply that he had no interest in furthering a relationship between the two of them, so—

'May I come in...?'

Stazy looked up sharply at the sound of her grandfather's cajoling voice. 'That depends on whether or not you're going to lie to me again.' She raised censorious brows.

He gave a self-conscious wince as he stood in the open doorway. 'I have explained the reason for that, darling.'

She nodded abruptly. 'And it was a completely

unacceptable explanation. I'm no longer a child you need to protect from the truth, Gramps!'

'So Jaxon has already pointed out to me,' Geoffrey acknowledged heavily.

Stazy stiffened defensively just at hearing Jaxon's name, let alone wondering in what context he might have made that remark. 'Was that before or after he left on his Harley?'

'Obviously before.' Her grandfather grimaced before glancing at the open suitcase sitting on top of her bed. 'What's going on, Stazy...?'

She drew in a deep breath even as she gave a dismissive shrug. 'I thought I might leave too, later this afternoon.'

His gaze sharpened. 'Leave? But—'

'You've said yourself that the danger is over now and your wound isn't serious,' Stazy interrupted firmly. 'And now that Jaxon has left there seems little point in my not joining the dig in Iraq as originally planned.'

The fact that she had taken out her suitcase before she even saw Jaxon leave wasn't something her grandfather needed to know! Even if Jaxon hadn't decided to leave, how could she possibly stay on at Bromley House after the events of earlier this morning? There was no way she could continue calmly working on the details for the screenplay with Jaxon as if nothing had happened between them.

Stazy was extremely reluctant to delve too deeply into her own emotions and find out exactly what that 'something' meant to her...

'Jaxon hasn't left completely, darling. He's just gone for a ride on his motorbike after being confined here for the past few days,' her grandfather told her gently.

'Oh.' Stazy felt the colour drain from her cheeks.

Geoffrey gave her a searching glance. 'Is there some-thing you want to tell me, darling...?'

The very last thing Stazy wanted to do was to con-fide in her grandfather about making love with Jaxon this morning! There was no way she could tell another man of the intimacies she and Jaxon had shared, and there wasn't the remotest possibility of her ever talk-ing to anyone about how those intimacies had resulted in her first ever earth-shattering orgasm!

Although she might not have any choice if, as her grandfather said, Jaxon had only gone for a ride on his motorbike and intended returning to Bromley House later this morning...

'No, nothing,' she answered her grandfather abruptly as she carefully avoided meeting his piercing blue gaze. 'As Jaxon isn't here at the moment I think I might follow his example and go out—go for a run along the beach,' she added lightly. 'We can discuss later whether or not there's any point in our bothering to continue with the research.'

Her grandfather looked puzzled. 'What do you mean?'

Stazy shrugged. 'You said the unauthorised biogra-phy on Granny was the reason this man from the past was able to track you down, so just think how much more exposed you will be if Jaxon goes ahead with the making of his film.'

'There is even more reason now for Jaxon to make his film, darling,' Geoffrey insisted firmly. 'Don't you see. It's the only way to dispel the myth and show Anastasia for the true heroine that she was,' he added when she still looked unconvinced.

Yes, Stazy did see the logic of that. Unfortunately. She had just been clinging to the hope—the slim hope, admittedly—that this recent scare might result in her grandfather rethinking his decision.

She gave an impatient shake of her head. 'As I said, we can all talk about this later—when Jaxon has returned from his ride and I've been for my run.'

Geoffrey nodded slowly. 'That would seem to be the best idea.' He turned to leave before turning back again. 'Are you and Jaxon still able to continue working together…?' he prompted shrewdly.

Stazy felt the colour warm her cheeks. Surely Jaxon hadn't—? No, of course he wouldn't. 'I can't see any reason why not, can you?' she dismissed lightly.

Her grandfather shrugged. 'You both seem more than a little edgy this morning…'

'Is that surprising when we've been cooped up here together for two days?'

And nights… Let's not forget the nights!

As if Stazy ever could…

'Geoffrey has gone to his bedroom to rest for a while.'

Stazy looked up from where she sat in the library, reading one of her grandmother's diaries. Well… 'reading' was something of a misnomer; even she knew she had only been giving the appearance of doing so. Because inwardly her thoughts and emotions were so churned up Stazy couldn't have concentrated on absorbing any of her grandmother's entries if her life had depended upon it!

Sitting down to eat lunch with her grandfather and Jaxon earlier had been something of an ordeal—so much so that Stazy had finally excused herself after eating none of the first course and proceeding only to pick at the main course for ten minutes or so, leaving the two men at the table to continue talking as she hurried from the room with the intention of escaping to the library.

She and Jaxon hadn't so much as exchanged a word during the whole of that excruciatingly awkward meal. That wasn't to say Stazy hadn't been completely aware of him as the three of them had sat at the small round table where she and Jaxon had eaten dinner together alone the past two evenings.

In the same room where Stazy had wrapped her legs around Jaxon's waist as he had pressed her up against the china cabinet and kissed her...

Her expression was guarded now as she looked across the room at him. 'Rest is probably the best thing for him.'

And what, Jaxon wondered as he came into the room and quietly closed the door behind him, did Stazy consider was the best thing for the two of *them*?

Logic said they should talk about what had happened between them this morning. Emotion told him that Stazy's feelings were so strung out at the moment that even to broach that conversation would only result in another meltdown—something she definitely wouldn't thank him for.

Because the two of them had spent the night in the same bed? Because of the intimacies they had shared with each other this morning? Stazy bitterly regretting the lapse?

Jaxon would like to think that wasn't the reason, but he still smarted at the way she had tried to push him out of the bedroom before anyone discovered him there. Admittedly, her grandfather had just flown in by helicopter, but even so...

Jaxon had had plenty of time to think things over during his long ride earlier. He had come to know Stazy much better these past three days, and knew without being told that with hindsight she would view her un-inhibited response to him this morning as a weakness. A weakness she had no intention of repeating…

His mouth thinned and his lids narrowed as she seemed to recoil against the back of her chair when he crossed the room in long, silent strides. He looked down at her frustratedly. 'Do you want me to make my excuses to Geoffrey and tell him that I have to leave unexpectedly?'

Her face was expressionless as she returned his gaze. 'Why on earth would I want to you to do that?'

'Maybe because you obviously can't stand even being in the same room with me any longer?' he reasoned heavily.

'Don't be ridiculous, Jaxon,' Stazy dismissed scath-ingly, inwardly knowing he was being nothing of the kind; she *did* find being in the same room with him totally overwhelming. The intimacies the two of them had shared this morning made it difficult for her even to look at him without remembering exactly where and how his lips and tongue had pleasured her this morn-ing…

'I don't understand you, Stazy,' he bit out bleakly. 'We're two consenting adults who chose to—'

'I know exactly what we did, Jaxon!' She stood up so suddenly that her chair tipped over backwards and crashed against one of the bookcases. 'Damn. Damn, damn, *damn*!' she muttered impatiently as she bent to set the chair back onto its four legs before glaring up at him. 'I don't want to talk about this now, Jaxon—'

'Will you ever want to talk about it?'

She gave a self-conscious shiver. 'Preferably not!'

Jaxon breathed hard. 'You're behaving like some outraged innocent that I robbed of her virginity!'

Maybe. Because in every way that mattered that was exactly how Stazy felt...

She had been completely in control of the situation when she had chosen her previous two lovers so carefully. And she had been physically in control too. The loss of her virginity to her university lecturer had been perfunctory at best, the second experience four years ago even more so.

The rawness, the sheer carnality of Jaxon's lovemaking this morning, hadn't allowed her to keep any of those barriers in place. He had stripped her down, emotionally as well as physically, and in doing so had sent all her barriers crashing to the floor, leaving her feeling vulnerable and exposed.

Oh, she didn't believe Jaxon had deliberately set out to do that to her. In fact she was sure that he had no idea of exactly what he had done. But, whether Jaxon knew it or not, that was exactly what had happened. And Stazy needed space and time in order to rebuild those emotional barriers.

She forced herself to relax, and her expression was coolly dismissive as she looked up at him. 'Is it being an actor that makes you so melodramatic, Jaxon?' she drawled derisively.

'It isn't a question of melodrama—'

'Of course it is,' she said easily. 'You're reading things into this situation that simply aren't there. Yes, our behaviour this morning makes it a little awkward for us to continue working together, but—as I assured my grandfather earlier—I'm more than willing to do my part so that we finish the research as quickly as possible. After which time we can both get back to our own totally different lives.' She looked up at him challengingly.

At this moment the only thing Jaxon felt more than willing to do was carry out his threat to put Stazy over his knee and spank some sense into her! Or at least spank her until there was a return of the warm and sensual Stazy he had been with this morning!

Not going to happen any time soon, he acknowledged as he recognised the same cool detachment in her expression that had been there when they'd first met just over six weeks ago.

'Shall we get on…?' She pulled her chair out and resumed her seat at the table before looking up at him expectantly.

Jaxon looked down at her exasperatedly. He felt the return of all his earlier frustrations with this situation, appreciating how it had all seemed so much simpler when he'd been riding the country roads on the back of the Harley.

Obviously, he had reasoned, Stazy had been understandably dismayed by the unexpected arrival of her grandfather. But once she got over her surprise Jaxon was sure the two of them would be able to sit down and talk about the situation like the two rational human beings that they were.

Somewhere in all that thinking Jaxon had forgotten to take into account that Stazy as a rational human being could also be extremely annoying!

To the point where he now felt more like wringing her delicate little neck than attempting to talk with her rationally!

Had he ever met a more frustrating woman?

Or a more sensually satisfying one…?

Jaxon had made love with dozens of women during

the past fifteen years, but he knew that none of them had aroused him to the fever pitch that Stazy had this morning. To the point where he had been teetering dangerously on the edge just from the touch of her lips and fingers—

That way lies madness, old chum, he told himself as he felt himself hardening again, just at thinking about having Stazy's lips and tongue on him there. *Total insanity!*

'Fine, if you're sure that's the way you want it,' he bit out tersely, and he moved to sit in the chair opposite hers.

It wasn't the way Stazy wanted it at all. It was the way she knew it had to be. For both their sakes...

CHAPTER ELEVEN

'So. The work's done, and we can both leave here later this morning…' Stazy kept her tone deliberately light as she looked across the breakfast table from beneath lowered lashes as Jaxon relaxed back in his chair, enjoying his second cup of coffee after eating what could only be described as a hearty breakfast. Unlike Stazy, who had only managed to pull a croissant apart as she drank her own cup of morning coffee.

No, that probably wasn't the best way to describe Jaxon this morning—after all, it was the condemned man who ate a hearty breakfast, and on the morning of his departure from Bromley House Jaxon appeared anything but that!

It had been a long and stressful week as far as Stazy was concerned, with the long hours she had spent alone with Jaxon in the library by far the biggest strain. But only for Stazy, it seemed. Jaxon, when he hadn't been secluded in the study with her grandfather, had been brisk and businesslike in her company, with not even a hint of a mention of the night they had spent together, let alone that conversation he had seemed so intent on the two of them having five days ago.

Her grandfather's return to London late yesterday

evening hadn't brought about any change in Jaxon's distant manner either.

Had she wanted it to make a difference?

Stazy had no idea what she wanted, except she knew she found this strained politeness extremely unsettling!

Jaxon shrugged the broadness of his shoulders in the dark grey tee shirt he wore with faded blue denims. The heavy biker boots were already on his feet in preparation for his departure. 'It's over for you, certainly, but the real work for me—the writing of the screenplay—is only just beginning.' He smiled ruefully.

Stazy's heart did a little lurch in her chest just at the sight of that smile after days of strained politeness. 'Can you do that while working on the pirate movie?'

He raised a dark brow. 'I appreciate it's a common belief amongst ladies that men can only concentrate on one thing at a time, but I assure you it's just a myth!'

Stazy felt warmth in her cheeks at the rebuke. 'I meant timewise, not mentally.'

'I'll cope,' Jaxon drawled as he studied her from between narrowed lids.

Was it his imagination, or did the fine delicacy of Stazy's features appear sharper than a week ago? Her cheekbones and the curve of her chin more defined, with dark shadows beneath those mesmerising green eyes?

Or was he just hoping that was the case? Hoping that Stazy had found the time the two of them had spent alone together these last five days as much of a strain as he had?

If he was, then he was surely only deluding himself—because there had certainly seemed to be no sign of that in her cool and impersonal manner towards him these past few days as the two of them had continued to work together on Anastasia's papers and diaries. *Frosty* had best described Stazy's attitude towards him. In fact this was the first even remotely personal conversation they'd had in days. At five days, to be exact...

'When do you expect to have finished writing the screenplay?'

'Why do you want to know?' Jaxon gave a derisive smile. 'So that you can make sure you're nowhere near if I should need to discuss it with Geoffrey?'

A frown appeared on her creamy brow. 'I was merely attempting to make polite conversation, Jaxon...'

Jaxon had had it up to here with Stazy's politeness! He stood up abruptly to move across the room and stare out of the window, the tightness of his jaw and the clenching of his hands evidence of his inner frustration. 'As we're both leaving here this morning, don't you think you should start saying what you really mean?' he ground out harshly.

Stazy watched him warily, sensing that the time for politeness between them was over. 'I thought, for my grandfather's sake at least, that the two of us should at least try to part as friends—'

'Friends!' Jaxon turned to look at her incredulously. 'You can't be so naive as to believe the two of us can ever be *friends*!' he bit out scornfully.

She knew that, of course. But nevertheless it was painful to actually hear Jaxon state it so dismissively.

'Friends are at ease in each other's company,' he continued remorselessly. 'They actually enjoy being together. And that certainly doesn't describe the two of us, now, does it?'

Stazy clasped her hands together beneath the table so that Jaxon wouldn't see how much they were trembling. 'I'm sorry you feel that way—'

'No, you're not,' he contradicted scathingly. 'You've wanted me to feel this way. Damn it, you've done everything in your power to push me away!'

She shook her head in denial. 'It was what you wanted too—'

'You have absolutely no idea what I want!' he rasped, grey eyes glacial.

'You're right. I don't.' She swallowed hard, her expression pained. 'Nor is there any point in the two of us discussing any of this when we will both be leaving in a few hours' time.'

'I'm not waiting a couple of hours, Stazy.' He gave a disgusted shake of his head. 'My bag is already packed, and I have every intention of leaving as soon as we've finished this conversation,' he assured her hardly.

He spoke as if he couldn't tolerate being in her company another moment longer than he had to, Stazy realised. It was a realisation that hurt her more than she would ever have believed possible...

Her chin rose proudly. 'Then consider it over.'

Jaxon stared at Stazy in frustration, knowing he wanted to shake her at the same time as he wanted to pull her up into his arms and kiss her senseless.

Where the hell was the vulnerable woman he had held in his arms all night long because she had been so worried about her grandfather? The same warm and sensuous woman who had responded so heatedly to his lovemaking the following morning?

Did that woman even exist or was she just a figment of his imagination...?

Jaxon had found himself wondering that same thing often when, time and time again, day after day, he had been presented with that brick wall Stazy had built so sturdily about her emotions.

And now, the morning of his departure, when he might never see Stazy again, really wasn't the time for him to try to breach those walls one last time...

He nodded abruptly. 'In that case...I hope you enjoy your trip to Iraq.'

Stazy no longer had any real interest in going on the dig she had once looked forward to with such professional excitement. No longer had any real interest in doing *anything* with the rest of her summer break now that the time had come to say goodbye to Jaxon... Which was ridiculous. He had no place in her life—had made it perfectly clear during these last few minutes that he didn't *want* a place in her life! So why should just the thought of Jaxon leaving, the possibility of never seeing him again, have opened up a void inside her she had no idea how to fill?

It shouldn't. Unless—

No...!

Stazy stopped breathing even as she felt the colour draining from her cheeks. She couldn't possibly have fallen in love with Jaxon this past week?

Could she...?

The threatening tears and the deep well of emptiness inside her just at the thought of never seeing him again after today told her that was exactly what she had done...

Had she ever done anything this stupid in her life before? Could there *be* anything more stupid than Dr Stazy Bromley, lecturer in Archaeology, falling in love with Jaxon Wilder, A-list Hollywood actor and director? If there was then Stazy couldn't think of what that something could possibly be!

The best Jaxon could think of her was that she had been a temporary and no doubt annoying distraction while he'd been stuck in the depths of Hampshire for a week doing research. She didn't even want to dwell on the worst Jaxon could think of her…!

She swallowed before speaking. 'I wish you an uneventful flight back to America.'

He gave a rueful shake of his head. 'It seems we've managed to achieve politeness this morning, after all!'

And if that politeness didn't soon cease Stazy very much feared she might make a complete fool of herself by giving in to the tears stinging the backs of her eyes. She stood up abruptly. 'If you'll excuse me? I have to go upstairs and finish packing.'

No, Jaxon *didn't* excuse her—either from the room, or from instigating the strained tension that had existed between the two of them these past five days. If it hadn't been for the buffer of Geoffrey's presence then Jaxon knew, research or not, he would have had no choice but to leave days ago.

Damn it, what did it take to get through—and stay through!—that wall of reserve Stazy kept about her emotions? Whatever it was, he obviously didn't have it…

He breathed his frustration. 'Will you attend the English premiere with your grandfather when the time comes?'

She blinked. 'Isn't it a little early to be discussing the premiere of a film that hasn't even been written, yet let alone made…?'

Probably—when the earliest it was likely to happen was the end of next year, more likely much later than that. Jaxon had arranged his work schedule so that he could begin filming *Butterfly* in the spring of next year, and after that there would be weeks of editing. No, the premiere wouldn't be for another eighteen months or so.

And there was no guarantee that Stazy would attend...

Did it really matter whether or not she went to the premiere? At best the two of them would meet as polite strangers, if only for her grandfather's sake. At worst they wouldn't acknowledge each other at all other than perhaps a terse nod of the head.

And that wasn't good enough, damn it!

'Stazy, I don't have to go back to the States for several more days yet if...'

'Yes?' she prompted sharply.

He shrugged. 'We could always go away somewhere together for a couple of days.'

Stazy eyed him warily. 'For what purpose?'

'For the purpose of just spending time alone together, perhaps?' he bit out impatiently. 'Something that's been impossible to do since your grandfather arrived back so unexpectedly.'

'Oh, I believe we've spent more than enough time alone together already, Jaxon!' she assured him ruefully.

He scowled darkly at her coolness. 'What have you done with that night we spent together, Stazy? Filed it away in the back of your mind under "miscellaneous", or just decided to forget it altogether?'

Stazy flinched at the scorn underlying Jaxon's tone. As if she could *ever* forget that night in Jaxon's arms! Or what had happened the following morning.

Or the fact that she had fallen in love with him...

A love Jaxon didn't return and never could. A love she wasn't sure she could hide if, as Jaxon suggested, they were to spend several more days—and nights!—alone together.

Even if she did feel tempted by the suggestion. More than tempted!

To spend time alone with Jaxon away from here, to make love with him again, would be—

Both heaven and hell when she knew full well that at the end of those few days he would return to his life and she to hers!

Stazy feigned irritation. 'Why do you persist in referring back to that night, Jaxon, when you've no doubt filed it away it your own head under "satisfactory, but could do better"?'

His eyes narrowed to glittering slits of silver. 'Are you talking about my performance or your own?'

Oh, her own—definitely. Twenty-nine years old, with two—no—three lovers now to her name. Two of which had definitely been less than satisfactory, and the third—Jaxon himself—who had shown her a sensuality within herself she had never dreamt existed. A sensuality that she knew she would drown in if she spent any time alone in Jaxon's company.

'Oh, don't worry, Jaxon. If anyone ever asks I'll assure them you performed beautifully!' she told him scornfully.

His nostrils flared. 'Stop twisting my words, damn it—'

'What do you want from me, Jaxon?' She gazed across at him exasperatedly. 'Yes, we spent a single night together, but we certainly don't have to compound the mistake by repeating it.'

He became very still. 'That's how you think of it—as a mistake?'

Her brows rose. 'Don't you?'

'I have no idea what the hell that night—and that

morning!—was all about,' he rasped impatiently. 'But no doubt you do…?' he prompted hardly.

Stazy shrugged. 'The result of a healthy man and woman having shared the same bed for the night. I'm sure I'm not the first woman you've spent the night with, Jaxon, nor will I be the last!'

He gave a humourless laugh. 'You really don't have a very high opinion of me, do you?'

She very much doubted that Jaxon wanted to know what she really thought of him. That he was not only the most heartbreakingly gorgeous man she had ever met—as well as the sexiest!—but also one of the kindest and gentlest. It had been that kindness and gentleness that had prompted him to spend the night in her bed so that she wouldn't be alone with her fears for her grandfather. The same kindness and gentleness that she now had every reason to believe would ensure he wrote Anastasia's story with the sensitivity with which it should be written.

'It's probably best if you don't answer that, if it's taking you this long to think of something polite to say,' Jaxon bit out impatiently, and he crossed forcefully to the door.

'Jaxon—!'

'Yes?' He was frowning darkly as he turned.

Stazy stared at him, not knowing what to say. Not knowing why she had called out to him—except she couldn't bear the thought of the two of them parting in this strained way. Couldn't bear the thought of the two of them parting at all! 'I never thanked you,' she finally murmured inadequately.

'For what?'

'For—for being there for me when I—when I needed you to be.' She gave a pained frown.

Jaxon stared across at her, having no idea what he should do or say next. Or if he should do or say anything when Stazy had made it so absolutely clear she wanted nothing more to do with him on a personal level.

He had thought of her, of the night the two of them spent together, far too often these past five days. And of what had happened between them the following morning. The woman Stazy had been that morning, the warm and sensual woman who had set fire to his self-control, had been nowhere in evidence in the days since. But Jaxon knew she was still in there somewhere. She had to be. That was why he had suggested the two of them go away together for a couple of days—away from Bromley House and the restraints her grandfather's presence had put on them. A suggestion Stazy had not only turned down, but in such a way she had succeeded in insulting him again into the bargain.

He straightened. 'Forget about it. I would have done the same for anyone.'

'Yes, you would.' She gave a tight, acknowledging smile.

Jaxon nodded abruptly. 'Your grandfather has my mobile and home telephone numbers if you should need to contact me.'

She frowned. 'Why would I ever need to do that...?'

No reason that Jaxon could think of! Nevertheless, it would have been nice to think there was the possibility of unexpectedly hearing the sound of Stazy's voice one day on the other end of the telephone...

This had to be the longest goodbye on record!

Probably because he wasn't ready to say goodbye to Stazy yet—still felt as if there was unfinished business between the two of them. A feeling she obviously didn't share...

Jaxon forced himself to relax the tension from his shoulders. 'No reason whatsoever,' he answered self-derisively. 'I'll go up and get my things now, and leave you to go and pack.'

'Yes.' The painful squeezing of Stazy's heart was threatening to overwhelm her. Not yet. Please, God, don't let her break down yet!

'I'll look forward to reading the screenplay.'

He raised mocking brows. 'Will you?'

'Yes,' she confirmed huskily.

He nodded briskly. ''Bye.'

Stazy had to literally drag the breath into her lungs in order to be able to answer him. ''Bye.'

Jaxon gave her one last, lingering glance before opening the door and letting himself out of the room, closing the door quietly behind him.

Stazy listened to the sound of his heavy boots crossing the hallway and going up the stairs before allowing the hot tears to cascade unchecked down her cheeks as she began to sob as if her heart was breaking.

Which it was...

CHAPTER TWELVE

Three months later.

'I HAD lunch with Jaxon today.'

Stazy was so startled by her grandfather's sudden announcement at a table in his favourite restaurant in London that the knife she had been using to eat the grilled sole she had ordered for her main course slipped unnoticed from her numbed fingers and fell noisily onto the tiled floor. Even then Stazy was only barely aware of a waiter rushing over to present her with a clean knife before he picked up the used one and left again.

Not only was Jaxon in London, but her grandfather had seen him earlier today…

After three months of thinking about Jaxon constantly—often dreaming about him too—it was incredible to learn that he was actually in London…

She moistened suddenly dry lips. 'I had no idea he was even in England…'

'He arrived yesterday,' her grandfather replied. He was now fully recovered from the gunshot wound and back to his normal robust self.

That was more than could be said for Stazy!

Oh, it had been a positive three months as far as her work was concerned. The dig in Iraq had been very successful. And when she'd returned to the university campus last month she had officially been offered the job as Head of Department when the present head retired next year. She hadn't given her answer yet but, having worked towards this very thing for the past eleven years, there seemed little doubt that she would accept the position.

No, on a professional level things couldn't have been better. It was on a personal level that Stazy knew she wasn't doing so well...

A part of her had hoped that time and distance would help to lessen the intensity of the feelings—the love—she felt for Jaxon, but instead the opposite had happened. Not a day, an hour went by, it seemed, when she didn't think of him at least once, wondering how he was, what he was doing. Which beautiful actress he was involved with now...

Since returning from Iraq she had even found herself buying and avidly looking through those glossy magazines that featured gossip about the rich and the famous.

If she had hoped to see any photographs of Jaxon then she might as well have saved herself the money—and the heartache!—because she hadn't succeeded in finding a single picture of him during the whole of that time. With a woman or otherwise.

The last thing she had been expecting, when her grandfather had invited her out to dinner with him this evening, was for him to calmly announce that Jaxon was in England at this very minute. Or at least Stazy presumed he was still here...

'Does he intend staying long?' she prompted lightly, aware that her hand was shaking slightly as she lifted her glass and took a much-needed sip of her white wine.

'He didn't say,' Geoffrey answered dismissively.

'Oh.' There were so many things Stazy wanted to ask—such as, how did Jaxon look? What had the two men talked about? Had Jaxon asked about her...? And yet she felt so tied up in knots inside just at the thought of Jaxon being in London at all that she couldn't ask any of them.

Although quite what her grandfather would have made of that interest if she had, after her previous attitude to Jaxon, was anybody's guess!

'He's finished writing the screenplay.'

Stazy's gaze sharpened. 'And...?'

Her grandfather smiled ruefully. 'And I recommend that you read it for yourself.'

She slowly licked the wine from her lips as she carefully placed her glass back down on the table. 'He gave you a copy...?'

'He gave me two copies. One for me and one for you.' Geoffrey reached down and lifted the briefcase he had carried into the restaurant with him earlier.

That second copy, meant for her, told Stazy more than anything else could have done that Jaxon had no intention of seeking her out while he was in England. And after the way the two of them had parted how could she have expected anything else!

Her grandfather opened the two locks on his briefcase before taking out the thickly bound bundle of the screenplay and handing it across the table to her. 'Read the front cover first, Stazy,' he advised huskily as she continued to stare at it, as if it were a bomb about to go off in his hand, rather than taking it from him.

Her throat moved convulsively as she swallowed hard. 'Have you had a chance to read it yet?'

Geoffrey smiled. 'Oh, yes.'

'And?'

'As I said, you need to read it for yourself.'

'If you liked it then I'm sure I will too,' she insisted firmly.

'Exactly how long do you intend to go on like this, Stazy?' her grandfather prompted impatiently as he placed the bound screenplay down on the tabletop, so that he could lock his briefcase before placing it back on the floor beside him.

Her hair moved silkily over her shoulders as she gave a shake of her head. 'I don't know what you mean…'

His steely-blue gaze became shrewdly piercing. 'Don't you?'

'No.'

'You have shadows under your eyes from not sleeping properly, you've lost weight you couldn't afford to lose—?'

'I think I picked up a bug in Iraq—'

'And I think you caught the bug before you even went to Iraq—and its name is Jaxon!'

Stazy's breath caught sharply in her throat at the baldness of her grandfather's statement, the colour draining from her cheeks. 'You're mistaken—'

'No, Stazy, you're the one that's making a mistake—by attempting to lie to someone who's had to lie as often as I have over the years,' he assured her impatiently.

She ran the tip of her tongue over her lips. There was a pained frown between her eyes. She knew from her grandfather's determined expression that he wasn't about to let her continue prevaricating. 'Is how I feel about Jaxon that obvious?'

'Only to me, darling.' He placed a hand gently over one of hers. 'And that's only because I know you so well and love you so much.'

She gave a shaky smile. 'It's probably as well that someone does!'

'Maybe Jaxon—'

'Let's not even go there,' she cut in firmly, her back tensing.

'I have no idea how long he'll be in England, but he did say he would be in London for several more days yet, so perhaps—'

'Gramps, I'm the last person Jaxon would want to see while he's here,' she assured him dully.

'You can't possibly know that—'

'Oh, but I can.' Stazy gave a self-derisive shake of her head. 'If you thought I was rude to him at our initial meeting then you should have seen me during those first few days we were alone together at Bromley House!' She sighed heavily. 'Believe me, Gramps, we parted in such a way as to ensure that Jaxon will never want to see me again!' Stiltedly. Distantly. Like strangers.

'Are you absolutely sure about that…?'

'Yes, of course I'm sure.' Her voice sharpened at her grandfather's persistence. Wasn't it enough for her to suffer the torment of knowing Jaxon was in England at all without having to explain all the reasons why he wouldn't want to see her while he was here? 'Feeling the way I do, I'm not sure it would be a good idea for me to see him again, either,' she said emotionally.

Her grandfather sat back in his chair. 'That's a pity…'

Her eyes had misted over with unshed tears. 'I don't see why.'

'Because when I saw him earlier today I invited him to join us this evening for dessert and coffee.' Geoffrey glanced across the restaurant. 'And it would appear he has arrived just in time to take up my invitation…'

* * *

Jaxon was totally unaware of the attention of the other diners in the restaurant as they recognised him. He walked slowly towards the table near the window where he could see Stazy sitting having dinner with her grandfather.

Even with her back towards him, Jaxon had spotted her the moment he had entered the crowded room; that gorgeous red-gold hair was like a vivid flame against the black dress she wore as it flowed loosely over her shoulders and down the slenderness of her back!

'Stazy,' he greeted her huskily as she looked up at him warily from beneath lowered lashes.

Her throat moved convulsively as she swallowed before answering him abruptly. 'Jaxon.'

Close to her like this, Jaxon could see that her face was even thinner than it had been three months ago—as if she had lost more weight. The looseness of the cream dress about her breasts and waist seemed to confirm that impression. 'I appreciate it's the done thing, when you meet up with someone again after a long absence, to say how well the other person is looking—but in your case, Stazy, I would be lying!' He almost growled in his disapproval of the fragility of her appearance. 'And I know how much you hate lies…'

Her cheeks were aflame. 'And what makes you think you're looking so perfect yourself?' she came back crisply.

'That's much better,' Jaxon murmured approvingly, before glancing across the table at the avidly attentive Geoffrey Bromley. 'When I asked about you earlier today your grandfather was at pains to tell me how happy and well you've been this past three months…' He raised mocking brows at the older man.

'Yes. Well. Family loyalty and all that.' Geoffrey had

the grace to look slightly embarrassed at the deception.
'I did invite you to join us for dessert and coffee so that
you could see Stazy for yourself. Speaking of which…
No, there's no need to bring another chair,' he told the
waiter as the man arrived to stand enquiringly beside
their table. 'I have another appointment to get to, so Mr
Wilder can have my seat.' He bent to pick up the briefcase from beside his chair before standing up in readi-
ness to leave.

'Gramps—'

'I believe you told me yourself weeks ago that you're a
big girl now and no longer in need of my protection…?'
he reminded her firmly, before bending to kiss her lightly
on the cheek. 'If you'll both excuse me…?' He didn't wait
for either of them to reply before turning and walking
briskly across the restaurant.

Yes, Stazy *had* told her grandfather that—but it had
been in a totally different situation and context from
this one!

That her grandfather had invited Jaxon to join them
this evening with the deliberate intention of leaving her
alone with him she had no doubt. Quite why he should
have decided to do so was far less clear to her…

Especially so when the first thing Jaxon had done
was insult her. And she had then insulted him back.
Some things never changed, it seemed…

Her own insulting remark had been knee-jerk rather
than truthful—Jaxon had never looked more wonderful
to her than he did this evening. His silky dark hair was
still shoulder-length, brushed back from the chiselled
perfection of his face, and the black evening suit and
snowy white shirt were tailored to the muscled width
of his shoulders and tapered waist.

He looked every inch the suave and sophisticated

actor Jaxon Wilder. Something Stazy had already noted the other female diners in the restaurant seemed to appreciate!

'So…' Jaxon had made himself comfortable in her grandfather's recently vacated chair while Stazy had been lost in her own jumbled thoughts.

'So,' Stazy echoed, her heart beating so loudly that she felt sure Jaxon must be able to hear it even over the low hum of the conversation of the other diners. 'You've obviously finished writing the screenplay.' She glanced down at the bound copy on the tabletop.

His gaze sharpened. 'Have you read it…?'

'My grandfather only just gave it to me, so no—' She broke off as she finally read the front page of the screenplay. 'Why is my name next to yours beneath the title…?' she asked slowly.

He shrugged those broad shoulders. 'You helped gather the research. You deserve to share in the credit for the writing of the screenplay.'

This explained why her grandfather had advised her to read the front cover when he gave it to her. 'I'm sure my less than helpful attitude was more of a hindrance than a help—'

'On the contrary—it kept me focused on what's important.' Jaxon sat forward, his expression intense. 'Look, do you really want dessert and coffee? Or can we get out of here and go somewhere we can talk privately…?' He absently waved away the waiter, who had been coming over to take their order.

Stazy raised startled lids to look across at Jaxon uncertainly, not in the least encouraged by the harshness of his expression. 'And why would we want to do that…?'

Jaxon cursed under his breath as he saw the look of uncertainty on Stazy's face. 'I've missed you this past three months, Stazy,' he told her gruffly. 'More than you can possibly know.'

She grimaced. 'Couldn't you find anyone else to argue with?'

He smiled ruefully. 'There's that too!'

She shook her head. 'I'm sure you've been far too busy to even give me a first thought, let alone a second one!'

'Try telling my female co-star that—we've had to do so many retakes because of my inattentiveness that I finally decided to give everyone the week off!' he muttered self-disgustedly.

Stazy blinked. 'The pirate movie isn't going well...?'

'Totally my own fault.' Jaxon sighed heavily. 'I haven't been feeling in a particularly swash or buckling mood.' He picked up one of her hands as it rested on the tabletop and lightly linked his fingers with hers. 'I *have* missed you, Stazy.'

She gave a puzzled shake of her head. 'How can you miss someone you didn't even want to be friends with the last time we were together?'

'Because friendship isn't what I want from you, damn it!' Jaxon scowled darkly. 'The fact that I asked you to go away with me for a few days should have told you that much!'

'You seemed to feel we had unfinished business—'

'I wanted to spend some time alone with you—'

'People are staring, Jaxon,' she warned softly, having glanced up and seen several of the other diners taking an interest in their obviously heated exchange.

'If we don't get out of here soon I'm going to give them something much more interesting than this to stare at!' he came back fiercely.

Stazy looked at him searchingly—at the angry glitter

in his eyes, the tautness of his cheek, his tightly clenched jaw and mouth. 'Such as…?' she prompted breathlessly.

'This, for a start!' He stood up abruptly, his hand tightening about hers as he pulled her to her feet seconds before he took her into his arms and his head swooped low as his mouth captured hers.

Stazy had always been reserved, never one for drawing attention to herself, but the absolute bliss of having Jaxon kiss her again—even in the middle of a crowded restaurant, with all the other diners looking on!—was far too wonderful for her to care where they were or who was watching.

She rose up on tiptoe to move her hands to his chest and up over his shoulders, her fingers becoming entangled in that gloriously overlong dark hair as she eagerly returned the heat of his kiss.

'God, I needed that…!' Jaxon breathed huskily long seconds later, as his mouth finally lifted from hers. He rested his forehead against hers. 'You have no idea—' He stopped speaking as the restaurant was suddenly filled with the sound of spontaneous applause from the other diners.

'Oh, dear Lord…!' Stazy groaned as she buried the heat of her face against his chest.

'Show's over, folks!' Jaxon chuckled huskily as he picked up the screenplay before putting his arm firmly about Stazy's waist to hold her anchored tightly against his side. The two of them crossed the restaurant.

'Sir Geoffrey has already taken care of the bill, Mr Wilder,' the *maître d'* assured him as they neared the front desk. He handed Stazy her black jacket. 'And may I wish the two of you every happiness together?' The man beamed across at them.

'Thank you,' Jaxon accepted lightly, and he continued

to cut a swathe through the arriving diners until just the two of them were standing outside in the cool of the autumn evening.

Stazy had never felt so embarrassed in her life before—at the same time she had never felt so euphorically happy. Jaxon had kissed her. In front of dozens of other people. Not only that, but he hadn't denied the *maître d*'s good wishes. Of course he had probably only done that as a means of lessening the embarrassment to them all, but even so...

Jaxon had kissed her! And she had kissed him right back.

'Do you think you could stop thinking at least until after we've reached that "somewhere more private"?' he prompted persuasively.

Stazy looked up at him uncertainly. 'Where do you want to go?'

He shook his head. 'Your apartment. My apartment. I don't give a damn where we go as long as it's somewhere we don't have an audience!'

Stazy gave a pained frown and looked up at Jaxon in the subdued light given off by the streetlamp overhead. 'I'm not sure I understand...' She was still too afraid to hope, to allow her imagination even to guess as to the reason why he had done something so outrageously wonderful...

'It's simple enough, Stazy. Your place or mine?' Jaxon pressured as the taxi he had hailed drew to a halt next to the pavement.

'I—yours,' she decided quickly; at least she would be able to walk out of Jaxon's apartment whenever this—whatever 'this' was!—was over. With the added bonus that when Jaxon had gone she wouldn't have to be surrounded by memories of his having been in her own apartment.

Jaxon opened the taxi door and saw Stazy safely seated inside, giving the driver his address as he climbed in to sit beside her. 'Come here—you're cold.' He drew her into the circle of his arms after he saw her give an involuntary shiver in the lightweight jacket she wore over the cream dress. 'Do you have to be anywhere in the morning?'

Her face was buried in the warmth of his chest. 'It's Saturday...'

'That doesn't answer my question,' he rebuked lightly.

Probably because Stazy didn't understand the question! Why did it matter to Jaxon whether or not she—? 'Oh!' she gasped breathlessly. She could think of only one reason why he might possibly want to know such a thing.

'Yes—*oh*,' he teased huskily. 'And before your imagination runs riot I have every intention of keeping you locked inside my apartment until you've listened to everything—and I do mean everything—that I should have said to you three months ago. That could take a few minutes or could take all night, depending on how receptive you are to what I have to say,' he acknowledged self-derisively.

Stazy moistened her lips with the tip of her tongue. 'Will there be any swashing or buckling involved in this...this locking me away in your apartment?' she prompted shyly.

Jaxon arms tightened about her as he gave an appreciative chuckle. 'I think there might be a lot of both those things, if it's agreeable to you, yes.'

Stazy thought she might be very agreeable...

CHAPTER THIRTEEN

'So.' STAZY stood uncomfortably in the middle of the spacious sitting room of what had turned out to be the penthouse apartment of a twenty-storey building set right in the middle of the most exclusive part of London. The views of the brightly lit city were absolutely amazing from the numerous windows in this room alone, and there appeared to be at least a dozen furnished rooms equally as beautiful in the apartment Jaxon had told her he only used on the rare occasions when he was in London.

'Let's not start that again, hmm?' Jaxon prompted huskily.

'No.' She smiled awkwardly. 'This is a very nice apartment. Does it have—?'

'Hush, Stazy.' Jaxon trod lightly across the cream carpet until he stood only inches in front of her. 'Tomorrow, if you really are interested, I'll give you the blurb that I received on this place before I bought it. But for now I believe we have other, more important things to talk about…'

'Do we?' She looked up at him searchingly. 'I have no real idea of what I'm even doing here!' She wrung agitated hands together. 'You had lunch with my grandfather today. Came to the restaurant this evening supposedly to join us for coffee and dessert—and then didn't even attempt to order either one of them. You then kissed me in front of dozens of other people after my grandfather left—'

Jaxon put an end to her obvious and rapidly increasing agitation by taking her in his arms and kissing her again.

More intensely. More thoroughly. More demandingly…

'You know,' he murmured several minutes later, as he ended the kiss and once again rested his forehead on hers, 'if I have to keep doing this in order to get a word in edgeways this is definitely going to take all night!'

Stazy gave a choked laugh. 'I don't mind if you don't…'

'Oh, I'm only too happy to go on kissing you all night long, my darling Stazy,' he assured her gruffly. 'Just not yet. First we need to talk. *I* need to talk,' he added ruefully. 'To make it completely, absolutely clear how I feel.'

She caught her bottom lip between pearly white teeth. 'How you feel about what…?'

'You, of course!' Jaxon lifted his head to look down at her exasperatedly. 'Stazy, you have to be the most difficult woman in the world for a man to tell how much he loves her!' he added irritably.

Stazy stilled, her eyes very wide as she stared up at him. 'Are you saying you love me…?'

'I've loved you for months, you impossible woman!'

'You've—loved—me—for—months…?' she repeated in slow disbelief.

'See? Totally impossible!' Jaxon snorted his impatience as he released her to step away and run a hand through the darkness of his hair. 'There are millions upon millions of women in the world, and I have to fall in love with the one woman who doesn't even believe I love her when I've just told her that I do!'

It was entirely inappropriate—had to be because she was verging on hysteria—but at that moment in time all Stazy could manage in response was a choked laugh.

Jaxon raised his eyes heavenwards. 'And now she's laughing at me…!'

Stazy continued laughing. In fact she laughed for so long that her sides actually ached and there were tears falling down her cheeks.

'Care to share the joke?' Jaxon finally prompted ruefully.

She leant weakly against the wall, her hands wrapped about her aching sides. 'No joke, Jaxon. At least not on you.'

'Who, then?'

'Me!' She smiled across at him tearfully. 'The joke's on *me*, Jaxon! I'm so inexperienced at these things that I— Jaxon, I fell in love with you when we were at Bromley House together. I didn't want to,' she added soberly. 'It just…happened.'

Jaxon began walking towards her like a man in a dream. 'You're in love with me…?'

'Oh, Jaxon…!' she groaned indulgently. 'There are millions and millions of men in the world, and I have to fall in love with the one man who doesn't even believe I love him when I've just told him that I do,' she misquoted back at him huskily.

His arms felt like steel bands about her waist as he pulled her effortlessly towards him, his gaze piercing as he looked down at her fiercely. 'Do you love me enough to marry me…?'

She gasped. 'You can't want to marry a doctor of archaeology?'

He nodded. 'I most certainly can! That is if you don't mind marrying an actor and film director?'

'Excuse me,' she chided huskily, 'but that would be a multi-award-winning Hollywood A-list actor and director!'

'Whatever,' Jaxon dismissed gruffly. 'Will you marry me, Stazy, and save me from the misery of merely existing without you?'

She swallowed. 'Being alone in a crowd...?'

'The hell of being alone in a crowd, yes,' he confirmed huskily.

Stazy knew exactly what that felt like. It was how she had felt for the past three months since she'd last seen Jaxon...

Tears welled up in her eyes. 'I've been so lonely without you, Jaxon. Since my parents died I've never wanted to need or love anyone, apart from my grandparents, and yet you've managed to capture my heart...' She gave a shake of her head. 'I love you so much, Jaxon, that these past three months of not seeing you, being with you, has been hell.'

'Hence the weight loss and lack of sleep?' He ran a caressing fingertip across the dark shadows under her eyes.

'Yes.' She nodded miserably.

'When you said a few minutes ago you were inexperienced in things, you meant falling in love, didn't you...?'

She gave a self-derisive laugh. 'I've never been in love. I've had two lovers, spent one night with each of them, and they were both utter disasters!' She grimaced.

'Forget about them.' Jaxon reached up and cradled

each side of her face, his love for her shining out of his liquid grey eyes. 'We're going to make love, Stazy. Real love. And it's going to be truly beautiful.'

'Yes, please...' she breathed softly.

'You haven't agreed to make an honest man of me yet,' he reminded her huskily.

'Is that a condition of the beautiful lovemaking?' she teased.

'I do have my reputation to think of, after all...'

Stazy laughed huskily at the dig as she threw herself into his waiting arms. 'In that case—yes, I'll marry you, Jaxon!'

'And have my babies?'

Babies. Not only Jaxon to love, but his babies to love and cherish... 'Oh, God, yes...!' she accepted emotionally.

'Then you may now take me to bed, Dr Bromley.'

She chuckled at his prim tone. 'If you think I'm going to sweep you up in my arms and carry you off to the bedroom before ravishing you then I'm afraid you're going to be disappointed!'

'I'll do the sweeping.' Jaxon did exactly that. 'You can do the ravishing.'

'With pleasure, Mr Wilder,' Stazy murmured throatily. 'With the greatest of pleasure.'

And it was.

Just over two years later...

'I'm truly impressed,' Jaxon murmured teasingly in her ear as the two of them stepped down off the stage to the rapturous applause of his peers, after going up together to receive yet another award for Best Screenplay for *Butterfly Wings.* 'I think you thanked everyone but the girl who made the coffee!'

'Very funny,' Stazy muttered as she continued to smile brightly for the watching audience as the two of them made their way back to their seats.

Jaxon chuckled. 'And after you were once so scathing about the length of the speeches made at these awards, too!'

'Just for that, you can be the one to get up to Anastasia Rose if she wakes in the night!' Stazy dropped thankfully back into her seat, her smile completely genuine now as she thought of their beautiful six-month-old daughter waiting for them at home. Geoffrey had opted to stay with his beloved great-granddaughter rather than accompany them to another award ceremony that he had declared would be 'far too exhausting at my age!'

'I'll have you know that Anastasia Rose and I have come to an arrangement—I don't wake her up if she doesn't wake me up!' Jaxon grinned smugly.

'Really?' Stazy turned in her seat to look at him. 'Does that mean we can have our own very private celebration later...?'

Jaxon chuckled. 'Insatiable woman!'

She arched teasing brows. 'Are you complaining...?'

'Certainly not!' He kissed her warmly—something he had done often during their two-year marriage, whenever and wherever they happened to be.

They both knew and happily appreciated that life, and love, didn't come any better than this...

* * * * *

Mills & Boon® Hardback

January 2012

ROMANCE

The Man Who Risked It All	Michelle Reid
The Sheikh's Undoing	Sharon Kendrick
The End of her Innocence	Sara Craven
The Talk of Hollywood	Carole Mortimer
Secrets of Castillo del Arco	Trish Morey
Hajar's Hidden Legacy	Maisey Yates
Untouched by His Diamonds	Lucy Ellis
The Secret Sinclair	Cathy Williams
First Time Lucky?	Natalie Anderson
Say It With Diamonds	Lucy King
Master of the Outback	Margaret Way
The Reluctant Princess	Raye Morgan
Daring to Date the Boss	Barbara Wallace
Their Miracle Twins	Nikki Logan
Runaway Bride	Barbara Hannay
We'll Always Have Paris	Jessica Hart
Heart Surgeon, Hero...Husband?	Susan Carlisle
Doctor's Guide to Dating in the Jungle	Tina Beckett

HISTORICAL

The Mysterious Lord Marlowe	Anne Herries
Marrying the Royal Marine	Carla Kelly
A Most Unladylike Adventure	Elizabeth Beacon
Seduced by Her Highland Warrior	Michelle Willingham

MEDICAL

The Boss She Can't Resist	Lucy Clark
Dr Langley: Protector or Playboy?	Joanna Neil
Daredevil and Dr Kate	Leah Martyn
Spring Proposal in Swallowbrook	Abigail Gordon

Mills & Boon® Large Print

January 2012

ROMANCE

The Kanellis Scandal	Michelle Reid
Monarch of the Sands	Sharon Kendrick
One Night in the Orient	Robyn Donald
His Poor Little Rich Girl	Melanie Milburne
From Daredevil to Devoted Daddy	Barbara McMahon
Little Cowgirl Needs a Mum	Patricia Thayer
To Wed a Rancher	Myrna Mackenzie
The Secret Princess	Jessica Hart

HISTORICAL

Seduced by the Scoundrel	Louise Allen
Unmasking the Duke's Mistress	Margaret McPhee
To Catch a Husband...	Sarah Mallory
The Highlander's Redemption	Marguerite Kaye

MEDICAL

The Playboy of Harley Street	Anne Fraser
Doctor on the Red Carpet	Anne Fraser
Just One Last Night...	Amy Andrews
Suddenly Single Sophie	Leonie Knight
The Doctor & the Runaway Heiress	Marion Lennox
The Surgeon She Never Forgot	Melanie Milburne

Mills & Boon® Hardback
February 2012

ROMANCE

An Offer She Can't Refuse	Emma Darcy
An Indecent Proposition	Carol Marinelli
A Night of Living Dangerously	Jennie Lucas
A Devilishly Dark Deal	Maggie Cox
Marriage Behind the Façade	Lynn Raye Harris
Forbidden to His Touch	Natasha Tate
Back in the Lion's Den	Elizabeth Power
Running From the Storm	Lee Wilkinson
Innocent 'til Proven Otherwise	Amy Andrews
Dancing with Danger	Fiona Harper
The Cop, the Puppy and Me	Cara Colter
Back in the Soldier's Arms	Soraya Lane
Invitation to the Prince's Palace	Jennie Adams
Miss Prim and the Billionaire	Lucy Gordon
The Shameless Life of Ruiz Acosta	Susan Stephens
Who Wants To Marry a Millionaire?	Nicola Marsh
Sydney Harbour Hospital: Lily's Scandal	Marion Lennox
Sydney Harbour Hospital: Zoe's Baby	Alison Roberts

HISTORICAL

The Scandalous Lord Lanchester	Anne Herries
His Compromised Countess	Deborah Hale
Destitute On His Doorstep	Helen Dickson
The Dragon and the Pearl	Jeannie Lin

MEDICAL

Gina's Little Secret	Jennifer Taylor
Taming the Lone Doc's Heart	Lucy Clark
The Runaway Nurse	Dianne Drake
The Baby Who Saved Dr Cynical	Connie Cox

Mills & Boon® Large Print
February 2012

ROMANCE

The Most Coveted Prize	Penny Jordan
The Costarella Conquest	Emma Darcy
The Night that Changed Everything	Anne McAllister
Craving the Forbidden	India Grey
Her Italian Soldier	Rebecca Winters
The Lonesome Rancher	Patricia Thayer
Nikki and the Lone Wolf	Marion Lennox
Mardie and the City Surgeon	Marion Lennox

HISTORICAL

Married to a Stranger	Louise Allen
A Dark and Brooding Gentleman	Margaret McPhee
Seducing Miss Lockwood	Helen Dickson
The Highlander's Return	Marguerite Kaye

MEDICAL

The Doctor's Reason to Stay	Dianne Drake
Career Girl in the Country	Fiona Lowe
Wedding on the Baby Ward	Lucy Clark
Special Care Baby Miracle	Lucy Clark
The Tortured Rebel	Alison Roberts
Dating Dr Delicious	Laura Iding